PRAISE FOR THE I

Here are some of the over 100,000 five star reviews left for the Dead Cold Mystery series.

"Rex Stout and Michael Connelly have spawned a protege."

AMAZON REVIEW

"So begins one damned fine read."

AMAZON REVIEW

"Mystery that's more brain than brawn."

AMAZON REVIEW

"I read so many of this genre...and ever so often I strike gold!"

AMAZON REVIEW

"This book is filled with action, intrigue, espionage, and everything else lovers of a good thriller want."

AMAZON REVIEW

DEAD AND BURIED
A DEAD COLD MYSTERY

BLAKE BANNER

RIGHTHOUSE

Copyright © 2024 by Right House

All rights reserved.

The characters and events portrayed in this ebook are fictitious. Any similarity to real persons, living or dead, is coincidental and not intended by the author.

No part of this book may be reproduced in any form or by any electronic or mechanical means, including information storage and retrieval systems, without written permission from the author, except for the use of brief quotations in a book review.

ISBN-13: 978-1-63696-024-1

ISBN-10: 1-63696-024-3

Cover design by: Damonza

Printed in the United States of America

www.righthouse.com

www.instagram.com/righthousebooks

www.facebook.com/righthousebooks

twitter.com/righthousebooks

DEAD COLD MYSTERY SERIES
An Ace and a Pair (Book 1)
Two Bare Arms (Book 2)
Garden of the Damned (Book 3)
Let Us Prey (Book 4)
The Sins of the Father (Book 5)
Strange and Sinister Path (Book 6)
The Heart to Kill (Book 7)
Unnatural Murder (Book 8)
Fire from Heaven (Book 9)
To Kill Upon A Kiss (Book 10)
Murder Most Scottish (Book 11)
The Butcher of Whitechapel (Book 12)
Little Dead Riding Hood (Book 13)
Trick or Treat (Book 14)
Blood Into Wine (Book 15)
Jack In The Box (Book 16)
The Fall Moon (Book 17)
Blood In Babylon (Book 18)
Death In Dexter (Book 19)
Mustang Sally (Book 20)
A Christmas Killing (Book 21)
Mommy's Little Killer (Book 22)
Bleed Out (Book 23)

[Dead and Buried (Book 24)](#)
[In Hot Blood (Book 25)](#)
[Fallen Angels (Book 26)](#)
[Knife Edge (Book 27)](#)
[Along Came A Spider (Book 28)](#)
[Cold Blood (Book 29)](#)
[Curtain Call (Book 30)](#)

ONE

Death was there. It was a palpable presence in the dark air.

Virgil Place, just south of Lafayette in Castle Hill, was a quiet, gloomy street, draped with orange light that drooped listless from cold, steel lamps bolted to old wooden telegraph poles. The houses, in funereal ranks, stood dark, with blind windows and silent doors which saw no evil and spoke no testimony.

The houses stood dark, all but number 2242. There, light flooded from the open door and bathed two patrol cars, parked with their red lights pulsing against the blacktop and the walls of the houses around them. There were also two ambulances and a crime scene van, and Frank the ME's beaten-up Ford.

I killed the engine of my old Jaguar, and Dehan pushed open the door. We ducked under the tape, and I stood a moment looking at the house. It was tall, narrow, and brown. The first floor and the upper floor were clapboard, and the basement, which rose about six feet above the ground, was faced in stone. The overall effect managed to combine sinister and grotesque in a way that was not easy.

To the right of the bow window, stone steps rose to a wooden door that stood open, allowing light to stream out onto the front yard and the street, casting shadows of plane trees and pin oaks across the asphalt. Light came also from the window, but the drapes had been pulled closed, so only thin gashes seeped out.

Dehan had stopped at the foot of the steps and was watching me with eyes that were still sleepy. There was a hint of a smile, but she hid it well.

"You solved it already?"

I glanced at her a moment and nodded.

"It was the butler. He did it in the ballroom with Miss Scarlet."

She turned and made her way up the steps, speaking over her shoulder.

"That butler is a hound dawg!"

The cop on the door nodded at us.

"Good morning, Detectives. Down in the cellar."

The house was standard 1930s. There was an entrance hall with stairs rising on the right to the upper floor, a passage leading to a kitchen in back, and a door on the left that led into a long living room and dining room. There was light coming from the upper floor, there was a lot of light coming from the living room, and, along the passage that led to the kitchen, there was a cellar door, and I could see there was light there too. I stopped and spoke to the uniform on the door.

"Was it you who responded to the 911?"

"Yes, Detective. Me and Gunther."

"All these lights were on when you arrived?"

"Yup, door was open like it is now. The light was on in the living room. Lights were on upstairs, and the cellar door was open, also with the light on. Just like it is now."

I nodded. "Thanks." I peered into the living room, muttering to Dehan, "That's a lot of light for one murder."

The living room was dusty. The armchairs and the sofa were expensive, over the top, overstuffed and in white leather. And old. They reeked of the '80s. They were arranged around a brass-and-glass table that had the stench of bad taste and padded shoulders.

The table at the far end had the same stench. It was a slab of inch-thick glass on a Greco-Roman stone pedestal. It also had a film of dust over it. Books on bookshelves that had been built into the alcoves to either side of the fireplace were an eclectic mix of hardbacks and paperbacks. I took in Tutankhamun, Plato, Carlos Castaneda, Agatha Christie, and Anais Nin at a quick look. I didn't see any plants or photographs.

At my shoulder, Dehan said, "Those are vinyls, and that's a record player."

I glanced at her, then followed her gaze. It was focused on a shelf, with maybe five or six hundred vinyl records to either side. The only one I could identify was *Sgt. Pepper's Lonely Hearts Club Band*.

Dehan hissed through her teeth and shook her head. "You don't think about nostalgia being nostalgic, but here it is, the eighties mooning over the sixties."

"In 2020. I wonder if it means anything."

She put a hand on my shoulder and smiled. "Everything means something, big guy."

She made her way to the cellar door, and I followed but took a quick detour to peer in at the kitchen. The lights were on there too.

The steps down to the cellar were narrow and made of bare concrete. The floor, nine steps down from the hall, was also concrete. But roughly at its center there was a hole, five or six feet long and about three feet wide. Arranged around the hole were Frank, the ME, Joe, the head of the crime scene team, one of his guys dressed in spaceman suits, and a platinum blonde in her midthirties, wearing a pretty red dress and high-heeled shoes to match. She was on her back, staring at the ceiling like it had astonished her somehow. She had two ugly wounds in her chest, and underneath her there was a large pool of blood that was still liquid, though it looked like it was beginning to congeal. By her side there was a spade.

Frank glanced at us and then back at the corpse.

"You're early. I thought you two only did cold cases. No one has failed to solve this one yet. You need to come back in about six months."

Dehan jerked her head at the spade.

"Was she digging the scene?"

Frank stared at her while she frowned into the hole in the floor. "That was in remarkably bad taste, Carmen."

She was still frowning at the contents of the hole when she answered, absently, "Yeah? You should see the living room upstairs. That really is in bad taste." After a moment she added, "Man."

I stood by her side and peered in. The hole was occupied by another body, though there wasn't much left of it. By the clothes it looked like a man, but most of the flesh had rotted away, and what hadn't rotted had become hard and leathery. Dehan said, "Corduroy jacket, flared pants, and that looks like a very wide tie."

Frank was still engaged with the platinum blonde. "I haven't got to him yet."

I grinned at Dehan. "Can you at least give us a time of death?"

He stared at me, genuinely shocked. "Oh, that's funny. That's very funny."

Dehan snorted a small laugh and muttered, "Asshole." Then to Frank, "Who is she?"

"No idea. No purse, no papers, nothing." He stood as a gurney rattled down the steps. "We'll see if we get a hit on her DNA or her prints."

I grunted. "Well dressed, tasteful, and in those heels. She didn't come here to do a spot of digging."

Dehan took a couple of pictures of her. Joe looked up from where he was hunkered over the spade, fitting it into a large plastic bag.

"The spade has what looks like fresh earth and concrete on it." He pointed at the edge of the hole. "And the chip marks and scratches look pretty fresh too."

I nodded and squatted down beside him to look at the edges

of the hole. He added, "No way of knowing how fresh, but days rather than weeks."

I looked up at Dehan and sucked my teeth. We stared at each other a moment, and she said, "So she came here to look at the hole, not to make it. Somebody else was making it."

I gave my head a small, sideways twitch that meant "maybe." "Or she was brought here to be shown it. Assumptions, but pretty safe ones, I'd say."

Frank snorted and smiled at Joe. "So that's how he does it. I've often wondered."

Joe chuckled as he stood with the bagged spade. "I've often wondered what a safe assumption was. Now I know. It's truly an education to see the master at work."

Dehan told them to take a hike, then scratched her head as she looked around the gloomy cellar. "So all the lights are on in the house, most of them, anyhow . . ."

I said, "So there was activity in the house, all over the house. We need to confirm that with the neighbor who called it in, that there are not normally this many lights on at night, or so much activity. But on the face of it, it looks like there was a lot of coming and going."

Frank climbed carefully down into the hole while we watched the gurney bearing the blonde's body clunk laboriously up the cellar steps. Dehan spoke absently, to herself.

"She came here to see something, or she came here for somebody to show her something." She blinked and turned to me. "We need to look at the rooms upstairs."

I gave my head a single nod. "To see if there has been a search. I agree." I jerked my chin at the floor. "It's been swept to conceal footprints. With that broom." I pointed at it in the corner, and Joe turned to look at it.

"Got it. We'll check it for prints."

I turned to Frank in the shallow grave. "But, who's this guy? He probably has no ID in that corduroy jacket of his, but what can you tell prima facie?"

I squatted down again, and Frank leaned over, gently feeling the corpse's pockets. Dehan said, "You know, Frank, I always wanted a partner who said things like 'whom' and 'prima facie.' It's what you expect from a homicide cop in the Bronx. Prima facie."

"You two do my head in. Nothing in his breast pockets." He spoke as he worked, "I can't imagine what it's like at home when you're not at work. Constant madness and intellectual rambling. Nothing in his hip pockets. My guess is the killer took it. He was methodical and cool." He glanced at me. "She used to be a nice, bright girl, John, and then you took her and made her like you. Nothing in his pants. Nothing in any of his pockets. No keys, no cash, nada."

I grunted. "What is he, forty?"

Frank sighed, like he was tired of hearing that question. "You know I can't answer that till I get him to the lab . . ."

I ignored the sigh and went on. "Okay, Frank, not more than not less than. He's not one and he's not a hundred. So close the gap for me. He's not twenty and he's not eighty . . ."

"Fine! He's not thirty-five and he's not sixty. That's as close as I'd like to get. A *big* margin of error either side of forty-five. On the face of it—prima facie, as you would say—he seems to have all his own teeth, hair was abundant and seems to be dark brown or black, clothes seem to be early eighties . . ." He inched around to look at the corpse's shoes. "Shoes look expensive. That's about all I can tell you, except that he was about six foot and male. Anything else will have to wait until I have examined him. Now let me work. I'll call you. Goodbye."

I looked at Dehan and made a face. "Sometimes, with Frank, he makes you feel unwanted. I don't know why."

Dehan shook her head and sucked her teeth. "Hold on with an open hand, Stone. He'll come back. Let's go up."

We left Frank sighing and Joe chuckling and climbed the stairs back to the ground floor. Dehan made for the stairs, but I wandered back down the corridor to the kitchen and peered in again. The light was on; there were a couple of cups on the draining board, plus a plate and a glass.

I stood staring at it a minute, then went back along the passage and stood in the living room doorway, with my hands stuffed in my pockets. Dehan hovered on the first step a moment, then dropped back down, came over to stand next to me, looking over my shoulder, and breathed in my ear, "Feeling nostalgic for your teens?"

"The eighties were not a great decade, Dehan." I stepped into the room and stood looking down at the vaguely grotesque sofa and armchairs. "I always wished I had been fifteen in 1965."

She leaned on the doorframe and frowned at me.

"Why fifteen? What happened in 1965?"

"Not a lot, aside from the first combat troops arriving in Vietnam, but it would have meant I was seventeen in '67, the Summer of Love, and I would have been eighteen and nineteen in '68 and '69 respectively. Which might have been fun." I shook my head. "When was the last time, do you think, that a person actually sat in this room and opened one of those books?"

She crossed the floor and stood in front of one of the bookcases, examining the tomes.

"There's a lot of undisturbed dust," she said. Then she turned to the drapes that hung across what I assumed were French doors onto the backyard. She peered through them a moment, then yanked them back and, using a slim flashlight from her pocket, examined the bolts that held the left-hand door to the jamb, top and bottom.

"Gunged up and rusted, and the lock is rusted too. No sign of scrapes or scratches."

I moved to a sideboard where there was a vase. When I lifted it, it left a clear ring in the dust, and inside it were the dried, rotted remains of some kind of organic material.

Dehan said, "I don't think this room has been disturbed for years."

I put down the vase and picked up a lamp in both hands,

looking at the ring it had left. "So what are we looking at, Dehan?" I put the lamp down. "Lay it out for me."

"No. Let's look upstairs first."

I wagged a finger at her. "There is a bathroom where we shall find toothpaste, barely used, and a single toothbrush. There will be minimal, basic toiletries. Three of the four bedrooms will have bare, unmade beds, empty or nearly empty closets, and about as much dust as this room has, but one of them will show signs of having been occupied by somebody with very basic, limited needs. My guess is that Joe might find traces of concrete and dirt in that room."

She stared at me for a long moment. "It's strange," she said. "When you do that, it makes me hot, but at the same time I want to slap you."

"Ja voll," I said, propelling her toward the stairs, "das is your Electra complex vontingk to kill unt luff at zee same time zee superior farzer figure."

"Now I only want to slap you."

Upstairs we found a bathroom and four bedrooms. The bathroom showed signs of minimal use, with a single, almost unused tube of toothpaste and a toothbrush. Dehan grunted at it, like she had expected more of it and it had let her down somehow.

"Whatever DNA we get from that will be ninety percent toothpaste."

She opened the cabinet, pulled out a hairbrush, and scowled at it. I frowned too. The strands of hair in it were long and blond.

"That doesn't make a lot of sense."

"No, Little Grasshopper, you mean it doesn't fit with the sense you are trying to make."

"It makes sense to you? Long blond hair makes sense to you? How?"

I shook my head, then shrugged. "A Hells Angel? She's got long blond hair. Let's look at the bedrooms."

It was pretty much what I had expected. The master bedroom and the two larger rooms had the mattresses wrapped in plastic sheets, the drapes closed, and a strong smell of mustiness, like the doors had not been opened in a long time. The drawers were largely empty, though some had bits of bedding in them that looked, felt, and smelled old and musty. The wardrobes were empty too.

The fourth room was smaller, the bed was made, and, as I had expected, there were noticeable remains of dirt and concrete on the floor, and particularly beside the bed.

Dehan stared around the room awhile, but it had little more to tell us.

"Okay," she said, "you predicted this. What does it mean?"

I rubbed my chin and offered her a smile that was more like a wince.

"It means there was somebody digging a hole downstairs."

"Don't be a wiseass, Stone."

"You didn't look in the kitchen."

"Okay, so what did you see in the kitchen?"

"Two cups, one plate, and one glass."

"So somebody was camped out here, digging a hole. Somebody else came to visit, had coffee, and got killed."

"Thumbnail sketch, yeah. But, question: How long does it take to dig a hole?"

She pulled down the corners of her mouth and hunched her shoulders.

"You have to break the concrete . . ."

"To do that you need a drill or a pickaxe."

She blinked a couple of times. "Right. Where is it?"

I stared down at the bed, trying to visualize the person who had slept in it. I spoke aloud, to nobody in particular.

"A man dies, presumably murdered, some time back, possibly as much as thirty-five or forty years ago. Somebody dumps his body in a shallow grave in the basement of this house and covers it in concrete. Years go by, maybe decades . . ."

My eyes drifted from the bed and then met Dehan's. We

stared at each other a moment. I said, "There has to be a record of this guy's disappearance. We need somebody on it."

She nodded and took up where I had left off. "Then, very recently, somebody moves into the house where his body had been hidden. Somebody with long, blond hair. Our Jane Doe? They are camping here, not living. And they don't start digging straightaway. They seem to be doing something else, we don't know what. Eventually, though, they dig a hole in the basement and find John Doe's body. But they don't pull it out or call the cops. They call Jane Doe, who shows up in a pretty red dress and heels. They have coffee, they take her down to the cellar, show her the body, and shoot her. Then they leave, taking the pickaxe with them, but leaving the spade, and all the traces of their having been here, including the toothbrush, plate, cup, and glass. Stone . . ."

"Seen this way it doesn't make a lot of sense."

"You're not kidding. Let's tell Joe to have a look up here, then we'll go talk to the neighbor. What was his name?"

TWO

"Mr. Frederick Garner?"

The red lights from the patrol cars pulsed on his face, making him look slightly diabolical. But when you looked more closely, he had prissy lips tightly pressed together, which, with his hands clasped over his belly on his doorstep, made him look more like a prim, disapproving daemon. He gave his head a little waggle and said, "Yes. You'd better come in. I made coffee, but it's probably cold by now." He turned and walked away into the hallway. "I was expecting you about an hour ago, to tell you the truth. I can make some more..."

We followed. Dehan answered.

"Thanks, but we won't take much of your time. A uniformed officer will be over later to take a detailed statement."

He led us through the hallway to what looked like a Hollywood depiction of a Victorian parlor. It had walls papered in blue-and-white stripes, wall lamps with elaborate glass shades, burgundy carpets, burgundy armchairs with white lace doilies, and shelves bearing many small statues of girls with long dresses, hats, and parasols.

He sat perched on the edge of the sofa, and Dehan and I each took an overstuffed chair. Dehan spoke.

"Could you walk us through what happened, Mr. Garner?"

He regarded her a moment with arched eyebrows.

"You want me to walk *you* through it now and then give your uniformed officer a detailed statement later. Is there anybody *else* you'd like me to tell about it? I mean, I have only been waiting two and a half hours to talk to somebody. And it *has* been a little traumatic!"

Dehan made a sympathetic face. "Only the judge and the jury when it goes to trial, Mr. Garner. We are very grateful, it's just that everyone has been very busy with, uh, you know, the dead bodies and things."

He caught the sarcasm and turned to speak at me.

"It was two a.m. and I couldn't sleep. Tinker Bell couldn't sleep either. She was up and about and all over the place..."

Dehan said, "Tinker Bell?"

He answered without looking at her. "My Burmese cat. I was going to call her Smoky, because she is like a little cloud of silent gray smoke, but Graham said it made her sound like a mackerel, and Misty was *so* corny, so I went for something completely different and settled on Tinker Bell."

"A good choice."

"How would you know? You haven't even seen her. Anyway, Tinker Bell was hyperactive and mewing incessantly. I am sure she could sense something coming. I got up several times to look out of the window, and I could see there was light pouring out of the house next door."

I asked, "What made you look out the window?"

He sort of sagged and sighed at the same time, rolling his eyes to look up at the ceiling.

"It's actually a good question, and the answer is I am not *entirely* sure. However, before you go accusing me of being a nosy parker, the fact is there *were* a couple of shouts, and before that there was the sound of a car arriving, then driving away, feet walking on the sidewalk, doors banging. Nothing, taken in *isolation*"—he leaned forward to give the word emphasis—"nothing that would make you stop and think, 'Oh, my goodness! Somebody is going to get *murdered* tonight.' But taken as a whole, there was an edginess to the night. And of course cats are *so* much more sensitive than you or I."

I nodded like I had noticed that myself. "So when you looked out of the window you noticed a lot of light coming from the house next door."

"Yes."

"Was that very unusual?"

"Oh, heavens yes! You don't see a soul in that house from one month to the next. It's a crying shame when you think that there are people sleeping rough in the parks because they have nowhere to live."

Dehan took a breath, held it, and creased the corners of her eyes.

"Yeah, getting a job can often solve that kind of problem. So, on those rare occasions when the owner of the house did show up, did you ever get to meet him, or her, chat over the fence, have coffee . . . ?"

Garner's face said Dehan was on a slippery slope into hell and he couldn't wait to see her lose her footing.

"We rarely chatted," he said to me, through tight, straight lips. "We were not that well acquainted, but we did exchange pleasantries on occasion."

Dehan asked, "Did he, she, or it have a name?"

"I must say," he said, dilating his nostrils and peering at her down his nose, "I find your manner quite . . ."

"You don't need to like me, Mr. Garner, only answer my questions. What's the owner's name, as far as you are aware?"

"Well, really!" He looked at me, and I shrugged and made a "whatcha gonna do?" face.

"*Her* name is April. April . . ." He thought for a moment. "One of those Scandinavian names, like Olafsen or Amundsen . . . Olsen! April Olsen. She's owned the house for *years*. Ten, fifteen years. Never lived here. I suppose she's from out of town. Always struck me as perfectly respectable. I suppose when she is in town she just pops in and stays at the house. Perhaps it's a pied-à-terre. I mean, how should I know?" He stared at me with wide eyes, like he had suddenly scandalized himself with an outrageous thought. "I am not my sister's keeper, am I? We knew each other to say hello over the garden fence, and comment on the weather."

Dehan found the photograph and showed it to him.

"Is this April?"

He sagged and sighed through his nose.

"Yes. Poor child. Perhaps if I had listened to Tinker Bell and called a little sooner . . ."

I considered him a moment, wondering how sincere he was, then shook my head.

"You can't hold yourself responsible, Mr. Garner. The only person who is to blame for April's death is the person who shot her."

He didn't look up from the picture.

"It's so hard to know, isn't it? Call too soon and you're a nuisance wasting precious police time, call too late and somebody dies because you were negligent and hesitant." Now he looked up. "Society codifies our behavior, but we take responsibility for it." He smiled, with a hint of nostalgia. "It was easier in the sixties."

Dehan glanced at him with interest. "Yeah? How's that?"

He regarded her with distaste, like she was the spinach he had to eat before he could have his ice cream.

"We didn't have the Hive Mind yet. The big thing now is being 'connected.' The big thing then was being free. Back then you made your choices and you took the consequences. Today we don't see it like that, do we? Society takes the consequences, so society takes the decisions." He held her eye a moment. "I'm saying I should have called the cops sooner, and screw how inconvenient it might be for you or my neighbors."

Something in what he said made me pause.

"She had the house for ten or fifteen years, you said."

"Yes, something like that."

"So I gather you've been here at least that long."

"Much longer. I have been here sixty-five years. I was born in the bed I sleep in now, and shall die in."

"So, who had the house before April did?"

"Oh." He drew back slightly and said again, "Oh, it stood empty for *years*! *Years!* It just stood there, empty."

"How long?"

"Oh, *years*! I don't know how long. Years."

Dehan bit back her irritation and said, "And before that?"

"Oh, my goodness..."

He sat back in the sofa and crossed one leg over the other. Tinker Bell, in the form of a small, gray cloud of fur, jumped up beside him and climbed on his lap. He stroked her absently, staring at the ceiling.

"I mean to say, we are going back, oh... maybe thirty or forty years. I can't even remember his name. A man, alone. He was divorced as I recall. I know he used to have parties, noisy ones."

"What happened to him?"

He shrugged and made a "how the hell should I know?" face.

"Happened? Nothing happened. He just left, went abroad or something. Whatever, it was a relief. Mommy was ill, poor love, and his parties were a terrible strain on her. After he left, the house stood closed for a long time. Then April started turning up. Sweet kid." His face darkened suddenly, and he turned to me. "That house has *bad* karma, you mark my words."

I grunted and thought for a while. Then I asked him, "Did you see any of the people coming and going last night?"

He shook his head. "No, not at all."

I went to stand, but Dehan said, "Mr. Garner, were you aware of any connection between April Olsen and the previous owner?"

He looked startled. "None at all, except that she must have bought the place from him, of course. But aside from that, not at all. I mean, they are separated by years, aren't they! He would be an old man by now."

She nodded once. "I guess he would." She put her hands on

her knees and glanced at me. I made a face that said I had no more questions, and we stood.

"Thank you for your time, Mr. Garner. As I said, an officer will come over later for your statement."

We stepped out into that darkest hour before the dawn and stood a short while on the sidewalk. We watched the gurney, with the soulless, dehumanized remains of what had once been a man, rattle down the path and get lifted, little more than a sack of bones, into the back of an ambulance.

Dehan jerked her chin at him. "You figure that's the previous owner?"

I made a face that was doubtful. "It's either him or somebody he didn't like much."

She grunted and nodded, then looked at her watch.

"Five thirty. Not much we can do for another three hours. What say we go home, have some breakfast, and chew the cud?"

"Sounds like a plan."

I stood a moment, looking at the yellow sheen of pallid light on the blacktop by the meat wagon, where the shadow of my ancient, burgundy Jag lay hunched, like a cat about to pounce, and Dehan, tall and slender, stood with her elbow on the roof, where the yellow lamplight reflected on her face. She was watching me. She smiled.

"You coming? Or are you going to stand there till the sun comes up?"

My footsteps were loud in the predawn dark. I opened the driver's door and climbed in, left the door open with one foot on the road. She got in next to me and slammed hers. I said:

"I want the financials for April Olsen." Then, "Why'd she buy the house?"

Dehan chewed her lip. I went on.

"She bought the house that she would eventually be killed in. She bought the house with a body buried in the cellar, under solid concrete." I tapped a tattoo on the wooden steering wheel. "She bought a house which, for years, she never really used for anything. If she wasn't going to live in it, she could have let it, or sold it, or advertised it on Airbnb. But she did none of those things. She sat on it and visited occasionally. Then, somebody . . ." I hesitated. "Somebody who wasn't wearing expensive high heels and a pretty dress dug up the corpse in her cellar, showed it to her, and shot her." I stared out at the gloomy street with its unhappy lamplight, then turned to Dehan, where that light looked beautiful laid across the planes of her face. "So for what purpose did she buy that particular house?"

Dehan shook her head. "I know right now you are all about asking the right questions in the right way. But what I think will help a lot more in formulating the right questions right now is four eggs, half a pound of bacon, rye toast, and a gallon of strong black coffee."

I pulled in my foot and let the door swing closed, turned the key in the ignition, and heard the big old engine growl.

"Once again, Dehan, you are right. And wise."

I pushed the stick shift into first and pulled away, accelerating steadily through second and third to fourth gear. We turned right onto a desolate Castle Hill Avenue and hit the gas going north, through Unionport, toward East Tremont.

After five minutes Dehan spoke suddenly.

"Okay, here's one. Was the body the reason she was killed?"

I nodded. "That's a good question. If we can positively connect her with the corpse in the shallow grave, that narrows our pool of suspects to somebody connected to them both."

"Probably."

I nodded. "Probably."

"The obvious question, which follows directly from that one . . ."

"Is, were they killed by the same person? Which leads inevitably to, was she looking for the corpse?"

She shook her head. "No. Somebody *else* was looking for the corpse, found it, and killed her. Besides, it's too pat. And it's full of holes."

"Like?"

"Like, A, how many years did she have the house before digging up the basement? Like, B, why the hell did she wait for somebody else to dig up the basement and then take *her* to see it? *In her own house!* Like, C, going back to what you said earlier, she buys the house and then doesn't use it. If she bought the house with the intention of looking for the guy who was buried in her cellar, why the hell did she never go to the house?"

We were quiet for a while, with only the hiss of the tires on the asphalt and the occasional car passing southbound to break the silence. I spun the wheel and crossed East Tremont onto Bronxdale.

"The fact is, Dehan, from the little we know so far, her behavior in relation to the house does not . . ." I grinned at her. "*Prima facie*, suggest somebody engaged in a desperate, life-and-death search."

"No." She pinched her ear and rubbed the lobe with her thumb. "Like you said, on the very little information we have so far. But, even so, the way she was dressed . . ."

"She had come from somewhere."

"Garner said there was a lot of activity, car doors, lights, people walking . . ."

I grunted and turned right onto Morris Park Avenue.

"Did they arrive together? That would mean . . ." I sighed. "Her killer is camped out in her house, looking for the corpse, he finds it, then arranges to meet her, at a restaurant or something, then brings her back, they have a row that involves storming all over the house, wind up in the basement, and . . . *bang!*"

She puffed out her cheeks and blew air.

"That makes some kind of twisted sense, I guess. It also begs the question—*all* these scenarios beg the question—what was it about him that made it so important to find his body?"

I slowed to turn onto Haight Avenue.

"And having found it, kill her and leave both bodies to be found. Along with all the killer's DNA and fingerprints in the bathroom and the bedroom." I pulled up outside our house, then killed the engine and the lights and sat staring out the windshield, down the long, quiet road. "That is very bizarre behavior, Dehan. I don't think I have ever seen anything like it. We need her financials. I want to know . . ."

She gently punched my shoulder with her right fist.

"Coffee," she said, "you want to know coffee, and bacon and eggs and toast. And then we'll request her financials and everything else. Then everything will make sense. You'll see."

THREE

The coffee and the bacon didn't help, but, back at the station house, getting on the phone and doing some research did. Dehan leaned back, ran her fingers through her hair, and said, "The property register lists the owner of 2242 Virgil Place as April Olsen, just like Garner said. She bought it from one Marie Braun in 2010. Marie Braun had, in turn, inherited it in 1992 from the previous owner, an Allan Bernstein, who had inherited it twelve years before that from his parents, Saul and Rebeca."

I wagged a pencil between my fingers for a moment.

"So the man Garner had talked about, who kept throwing noisy parties, was Allan Bernstein. Does that make the woman who inherited it and sold it to April Olsen his wife?"

"We should find out. What about you?"

"April Olsen has no listed next of kin except for her parents."

She frowned. "Really? At, what was she, thirty-five? That's unusual."

"Thirty-six. Unmarried, no kids. Her parents are Olsen and Olsen, a firm of civil rights attorneys in DC. I tried calling a couple of times but I just get the answering service. They're in the office from ten a.m."

She snorted. "I like the hours for fearlessly defending the rights of the marginalized and underprivileged."

"Yeah." I glanced at my watch. "I'll give them another try in ten minutes. We should go and see them. I don't want to give them that kind of news over the phone. Aside from that, I'd like to get a handle on April Olsen. Maybe they can tell us what the deal was with that house."

She nodded. "We should also go talk to Marie Braun about her benefactor." She thought for a moment. "We have to be careful. We don't know if the guy in the cellar was her benefactor or her benefactor's victim, or had nothing at all to do with her benefactor. We also don't know if her benefactor was her ex, her brother . . ." She shook her head. "We don't know what that relationship was."

I nodded, grunted, chewed my lip, and went to get some coffee-like liquid from the coffee-like liquid machine. When I got back I put a cup in front of Dehan, dropped into my chair, and picked up the phone. It rang six times, and I was about to hang up when a voice that was educated but trying to sound like a man of the people said, "Yeah, Olsen and Olsen, Greg speaking. What can I do for you?"

"Good morning, Greg, this is Detective John Stone of the New York Police Department. I need to speak to either Mr. or Mrs. Olsen. It is a matter of some urgency."

"Oh, I see. Can I help in any way, Detective?"

"Not unless you are either Mr. or Mrs. Olsen."

"They are not here right now. They usually come in a bit later."

"I'll tell you what we are going to do. I am going to make an appointment with you to see them at four o'clock this afternoon. I'm going to leave New York a little before noon, so I would expect to be in DC before four. I have the office address, so my partner and I will be there at four o'clock or perhaps a little before. Will that be a problem?"

"Well, no, but as I say . . ."

"Just contact them and tell them we're coming and that it is very important. Can you do that, Greg?"

"Yeah, sure, I'll do that. No worries."

He sounded like I had spoiled his cappuccino. I smiled and hung up.

"You think we have time to go and see Mrs. Braun before we head off for DC?"

She was nodding at her computer screen.

"Way ahead of you, big guy." She tossed me a glancing smile. "Joyful Autumns Retirement Home, Waldo Avenue in Fieldstone. That's where I'm going to send you when you start dribbling."

"I'll have fed you to the hounds long before that happens. Where, pray, is Fieldstone?"

"It is a privately owned, affluent neighborhood in Riverdale."

"Our Riverdale?"

"Cross Bronx Expressway, Henry Hudson Parkway, fifteen minutes. The way you drive, maybe fourteen and a half."

"Mad, bad, and dangerous. That's me. It's just her?"

"Apparently, I don't know. There may be a husband and kids." She shrugged. "Let's go find out."

―――

THE JOYFUL AUTUMNS Retirement Home was a converted mansion set among leafy meandering lanes that cocked a well-heeled snook at the grid system, presumably on the grounds that the people who inhabited Fieldstone were far too rich to need to get anywhere in a hurry, much less by means of a boring, straight line. The path of value, the winding, overgrown byways seemed to say, is the one that wends. And I found myself, in my inner being, agreeing with them as I wended my way.

We came at last to the large, Greco-Roman gate that gave access to the short, half-moon driveway and eased in. A flight of granite steps rose to a Georgian doorway that looked down its fine nose at us from beneath a discrete Palladian arch. I killed the engine, and Dehan sat a moment, with her arm resting on the open window, looking up at the grand, elegant entrance.

"Mrs. Braun is clearly not short of cash."

I gave my head a small tilt to one side. "Or at least, whoever is paying for her to be here is not."

She regarded me a moment, pursing her lips, then climbed out of the car. I followed suit, and we ascended the ancient steps to the ancient door.

The entrance hall was the size of a small aircraft carrier. On the left was a long, low counter in dark wood. Behind that were a couple of pretty women with efficient smiles and detached eyes. On the right, the original doors had been removed from what had probably been the ballroom and replaced with institution fire doors that were remarkable for the level of depressing ugliness which they achieved. Ahead, a broad flight of wooden stairs divided into two open ram's horns and rose to a galleried landing on the next floor.

Dehan turned and made her way to the desk and leaned on it with both hands.

"Good morning, I am Detective Dehan, and this is my partner, Detective Stone." She showed the smiling woman her badge. "NYPD. We would like to speak to Mrs. Braun. We called . . ."

"Yes, I remember, you called earlier." The smile didn't falter. "I am not sure how helpful you'll find her."

She stood and came around the counter, and we followed her toward the ugly fire doors. "She has periods where she is quite lucid and charming. She's a highly educated woman, you know. But at other times she is away with the fairies, I'm afraid."

We went through the doors into a room that wasn't so much large as vast. The floor alternated square and round mosaics in a way that must have been either spectacular or nauseating when you were dancing a polka. A series of Greco-Roman columns framed what had once probably been the dance floor and sectioned off the perimeter of the room where you could stand

and drink champagne while you conspired to commit murder and treason. The far wall was all a series of French doors that opened onto a spectacular rose garden with what looked like a genuine Italian Renaissance fountain, only the naked god had no water spouting from his mouth. Or anywhere else, for that matter.

I put my fingers on the smiling woman's elbow to slow her down a little. She turned her smile on me and came almost to a halt.

"Is there any family? Who put her in here? Who pays the bills?"

She spoke softly, as though I was likely to embarrass myself and she was trying to save me from such a fate.

"Um, we don't really inquire into our guests' lives, Detective. But I can tell you that Mrs. Braun's bills are paid from an ample trust fund." She smiled like she'd pulled off a difficult trick. "She is well provided for." She gave a pretty laugh and started to walk again. "As to who 'put her in here'"—she stressed the words, somehow managing to suggest there were inverted commas around them—"nobody 'put her in here.' She chose to reside with us because her mother had before her. She came in with her two daughters, and they visit her regularly, every weekend, like clockwork."

Dehan said, "And Mr. Braun?"

"I'm afraid I have no idea. You'll have to ask her."

We had been walking hesitantly, talking, and now we arrived at a round table beside an open French door. There was a woman seated at it, watching us. She was only in her seventies, but her hair was extremely white and soft and gave her the appearance of being older than she really was. She had very blue eyes, a string of very good pearls, and wore a very fluffy, very pink cardigan. She was watching us with amused, ironic eyes and ignoring the smiling receptionist, who now said, "Mrs. Braun, these are Detectives Carmen Dehan and John Stone, from the New York Police Department. They would like to ask you a few questions."

We were pulling our badges, but she shook her head and waved a hand.

"I don't need to see your credentials. Sit down. I have the early onset of Alzheimer's, chances are in half an hour I won't remember you showed me. I have better periods and worse periods. You're lucky you caught me at a better period right now, but I can't guarantee how long it will last." She grinned at Dehan. "And if my daughters have been up to any kind of shenanigans, I can't promise I won't pretend to be having a bad spell either."

Dehan returned the grin as we sat. "We're not interested in your daughters, Mrs. Braun."

"Of course not. Why should you be? So, in what way do you think I can help you, then?"

I said, "In 1992, you inherited a house in New York."

Her eyebrows rose high on her forehead. "Good Lord! Yes, I did. Was that 1992? It seems like yesterday. What of it?"

"We'd like to know who you inherited it from."

She frowned hard, not trying to remember but trying to understand. "Are you serious? I inherited it from my ex-husband, of course."

I leaned forward, with my elbows on the table. "What was his name?"

"Allan, Allan Bernstein. Don't tell me the bastard has shown up alive! Why, he must be in his eighties by now!"

Dehan glanced at me. I went on, "I am sorry, Mrs. Braun, I know this must be distressing . . ."

"It's not distressing. It's interesting. I want to know what the hell is going on and why you're asking me questions about Allan "

Dehan cut in. "We are a cold-case team, Mrs. Brau . . ."

"Really? You try to solve old cases? How is Allan a cold case? He was a bastard in many ways, but he always honored his obligations."

Dehan went on. "We have a . . ." She hesitated. "We have a set of circumstances which we don't fully understand, and anything you can tell us would be hugely helpful. You said, 'Don't tell me the bastard has shown up alive!' What did you mean by that? How did he die?"

She shook her head. "Well that's just it. He didn't. That is, he may have done. I don't know. He went off to New Mexico to carry out his stupid experiments with mind-altering drugs, as if that hadn't all been done already in the sixties, and then he moved on to Mexico and disappeared. I suppose he found some gorgeous Mexican girl, blew his mind with her, *man*, and got killed by her boyfriend or father or cousin or something. Anyway, after seven years I filed to have him declared dead and I inherited the house and what little money he had left. I already had the trust fund for myself and the kids, and then there are the royalties from the books he wrote. He didn't leave me badly off."

I took a moment to assimilate this. "Forgive me, this may seem like an absurd question, but are you certain that he went to New Mexico?"

"Yes, of course I'm certain. We were divorced at the time of course, and we were not living together, but we stayed in touch and he wrote me from there, and then he telephoned me."

Dehan was screwing up her brow, trying to get a handle on what she was hearing. "He wrote to you and telephoned you. What about?"

Mrs. Braun gave a small sigh through her nose and flopped back in her chair, with her hands in her lap.

"He was such an egotist. He was a brilliant man. He lectured at Columbia in psychology and social sciences, you know? He could have been outstanding, an eminence in his field. But with him it was like with so many artists. What they do is all about *them* instead of the subject. Allan had absolutely *no idea* of the impact he had on the people around him. More to the point, he didn't *care*. That was why I divorced him in the end. I was living with him and so was he. I was just somebody to listen to his theories and hear how brilliant he was. That was bad enough, but when he started throwing crazy, druggy parties and having affairs with young undergraduates, that was the last straw. I packed my bags and left. He couldn't understand it."

Not sure if she had slipped into one of her "not so good" periods, I hesitated. "So, the phone call?"

She laughed. "He tried to tell me that he was researching the impact of mind-altering aphrodisiacs on consciousness. He believed they freed the mind from inhibition and made you more creative. He encouraged me to experiment—him and that friend of his. What was his name? Anyway, I told him experimenting was not just trying things out to see what happened, but developing a theory, from there a hypothesis, and then a set of variables in a controlled environment. Of course it did no good. Even after I had left him he continued to write to me about his ideas, which were increasingly insane, and when he was drunk or stoned or high, he would telephone me. He said I was the only woman he knew who was intelligent enough to understand him. I told him I was the only woman he knew stupid enough to listen to him."

"So when he telephoned you, it was from Mexico . . . ?"

"New Mexico. He wrote to me from Mexico telling me he had been trying peyote buds and he was sure they provided a portal to a parallel reality of the mind. Some such garbage. But he needed the guidance of a shaman to help him navigate that reality. There were none in New Mexico, so he was going to move on to Mexico. A day or so after that he telephoned me and told me the same crap. I told him he was going to lose his place at Columbia. He said he didn't care. He knew he was on the brink of a discovery that would change the world. About a week later he sent me another letter from Mexico, saying he had found the name of an old brujo who was going to guide him in the use of peyote and he was going to write a book about it. That was the last I ever heard from him. I suppose he found some gorgeous Mexican girl, blew his mind with her, *man,* and got killed by her boyfriend or father or cousin or something."

I glanced at Dehan. She had caught the exact repetition too. I figured we didn't have too long.

"Have you any photographs of Allan, Mrs. Braun?"

"No. Why?" She laughed. "Don't tell me the bastard has shown up after all these years!"

I smiled. "No, not as such. Thank you so much for your time, Mrs. Braun. You have been very helpful."

She frowned, and for a moment there was distress in her eyes.

"I have?" And then, "I'm not exactly sure who you are."

Dehan took her hand and smiled. "We were just here to check you were okay," she said. Mrs. Braun smiled back, uncertainly.

"Are you Mexican?"

"A bit?"

"Did you kill Allan?"

"No, that wasn't me."

"Oh, okay. Thanks for looking in."

"You bet."

At the reception desk we paused to ask for Mrs. Braun's daughters' contact details. The woman was still smiling prettily but said, "I can't do that."

Dehan smiled back in the same way and said, "We need to notify them of the death of their father."

"Oh . . . What I *can* do is get them to contact you on an urgent matter. How will that do?"

I told her it would do fine, and we stepped out into the morning sunshine.

FOUR

Dehan sat on the hood of my old Jag and made a call on her cell phone. I opened the driver's door and leaned on it, watching her. Dappled shadows of leaves moved across a warm patch of sun on her back.

"Yeah, good morning, this is Detective Carmen Dehan of the NYPD. Can you put me through to your personnel department?" She turned and looked at me and smiled. Then she looked away at the treetops. "Yeah, good morning. This is Detective Dehan of the NYPD. I wonder if you can help me out here. Back in . . ." She did some quick mental arithmetic: 1992 minus seven. "1985 you had one Allan Bernstein working as a professor in your Psychology and Social Sciences Department."

She made eye contact with me again, nodding slightly while she listened.

"That's the guy," she said. "Now, I am going to need to contact anyone in his department, or the university for that matter, who might have known him back then, who had contact with him, and, not least, anyone who might be able to identify him."

She smiled and rolled her eyes at me. Then said, patiently, "Well, we don't know, that's why we need somebody who can identify him." She listened a little longer, then said, "That would be very helpful. This number, yes. Thanks."

And she hung up.

"She's going to talk to the head of psychology and social sciences. She knows he knew Allan pretty well. Apparently he's a bit of a legend. She'll call me and arrange a meeting. If nothing else, we'll find out if the guy in the cellar is indeed Allan Bernstein."

"Good. Let's make a move and get ourselves over to DC. I am very curious to talk to the Olsens."

I climbed in and slammed the door, waited for Dehan to get in the other side, then fired up the big old engine. As we rolled out of the drive, I glanced at Dehan.

"It would have been interesting to hear what Mrs. Braun thought of April, whether they got to know each other. But I felt she was drifting a bit by the time we left."

"She was away." She was quiet for a bit, with her elbow on the open window and the wind pulling strands of hair across her face. Finally she said, "So who's the guy in the cellar?"

I drummed the steering wheel, thrust out my lip, made a few "hmmm . . ." noises, and watched the leafy lane unfold before me. "Logic dictates," I said at last, "that the man in the cellar is either Allan Bernstein or the reason Allan Bernstein went to Mexico."

She nodded. "It is not unheard of for people who kill other people to head south. It's also not unheard of for people to die at crazy parties. Sometimes it's accidental, other times not so much. Sharon Tate springs to mind."

"You have people's deepest, darkest desires being unleashed on the one hand, and their inhibitions being suppressed on the other. It's a bit like taking a four-year-old little Oedipus, putting him in the body of the Hulk, handing him an axe, and saying, 'Look, there's your mom, and that guy with her? That's your dad.'"

She narrowed her eyes at me. "You're a very strange man sometimes, Stone. You have a dark mind."

"All mind is dark, Dehan. That's why people like Allan Bernstein go so crazy studying it. It's a messy, sticky spider's web. And, having said that, I will add that I do not share the popular repudiation of Freud and his darker theories. People react to Freud exactly as he would have expected them to, with distaste and fear. But I think he had his finger on the pulse and knew a thing or two."

She let me finish, then said, "So you think the guy in the cellar is somebody Bernstein mistook for his father while he was out of his mind on some hallucinogen?"

"No, Dehan. I was merely illustrating the kind of dark, psychic impulses that can be released when people combine hallucinogenic drugs, marijuana, and alcohol. At our core, if you strip away all the mental systems we have in place to control our behavior, we are little more than voracious, violent predators."

"Well, you're preaching to the choir there, big guy. Our inhibitions don't come preloaded, that's for sure. They need to be installed, and a puff of weed and a snort of coke will go a long way to wiping your hard drive."

After a while she added, "So, he's having some kind of crazy party where his guests are dining with the Mad Hatter and dancing with the Pied Piper of Hamelin to the tunes of John, Paul, George, and Ringo. We know Allan was having affairs. So maybe he came across the guy in the basement having his consciousness elevated by his, Allan's, current babe. He went into a drug-induced psychotic break and killed him."

I shrugged. "Why didn't current babe call the cops?"

"She was going to, but Allan killed her too."

"Where is her body?"

"In the grave next to his."

"That's possible. Get Joe, will you?"

She dialed the lab and put it on speaker.

"Hey, Carmen. Does John know you're calling me? I won't tell my wife if you don't tell him."

I snarled, "Shut up, Joe. Stick to your green pastures, you ain't cut out for these badlands. This is man's territory."

Dehan laughed and punched my right shoulder. "Asshole!"

"Listen. Can you deploy a GPR in the basement at Virgil Place? We're just talking this through and there's an outside chance there is another body there."

"Yeah, we can do that. We're going over the upstairs of the house and we've found a few partials and a few hairs in the bed. We might be able to get something from the toothbrush and the glass too. I'll let you know."

I hung up. "So, he shoots his two victims, locks them in the cellar, and goes back to his party. When he's got over his hangover the next day, or the day after that, what does he do? He goes back down to the cellar and he has to dig through a thick layer of concrete, twice, and then dig into the soil, before dumping the bodies in. But having done that, his troubles are not yet over, because he now has to bury them and cover them in fresh concrete. That is not an easy undertaking."

She grunted and fingered hair from her face. "And the only person who might have found evidence of it, when she bought the house, wound up dead beside an uncovered grave."

"It's a brainteaser."

We didn't talk much for the rest of the journey, and arrived at D Street NE, in DC, at ten minutes before four. The address was a two-story gray brick building on the corner, with plate glass windows and white, high-gloss woodwork. A brass plaque beside the door said this was the offices of Olsen and Olsen, human rights lawyers specializing in immigration, refugees, and constitutional law.

I killed the engine, and we sat a moment looking at the place. The sun was reflected on the glass so you couldn't see much inside, but it didn't look like there was a lot to see either. Dehan leaned across me to peer in.

"It's four o'clock and they're already closed? When do these guys work?"

"Let's go and find out."

We climbed out and crossed the sidewalk to the smoked, plate glass doors. They were open, and we pushed through. A pretty girl in a smart suit looked up from her computer behind a polished oak reception desk and smiled, with her head tilted on one side.

"I'm sorry," she said, like she really didn't care at all, "we're closed. Can you phone tomorrow morning to make an appointment?"

I advanced to the desk and stood looking down at her.

"Do I look to you like I need help with immigration?"

She shook her head and shifted pretty, catty eyes to look at Dehan.

"No," she said, "but she might."

"We're cops," Dehan growled. "We have an appointment to see Mr. and Mrs. Olsen. Tell them we're here."

She gave a private little smile and picked up the internal phone. After a moment she said, "Tell Mr. and Mrs. O that their four o'clock is here." Then, after a moment, she pressed the receiver to her chest and said, "Can I see some ID, please?"

We showed her our badges, and she examined them with care, without touching them. Then she winked up at me and said, "Thank you, John." Into the receiver she said, "Okay. I'll send them up."

She hung up and pointed at a flight of stairs over on her right. "Up there. Greg'll show you to their offices."

The stairs were narrow and carpeted, and the loose boards beneath the blue carpet squeaked and complained as you trod on them. At the top there was a spacious landing with a small kitchenette, a john, a cubicle that pretended it was an office, and then two large, important-looking walnut doors, each with a brass plaque, one of which read May Olsen and the other Geoffrey Olsen.

Greg was standing in the middle of the floor in a white shirt with a burgundy stripe. He wasn't sure whether to smile or not, so he just looked like his constipation was giving him trouble.

He said, "Detectives."

I said, "Greg."

And Dehan said, "Which office are they in?"

"I am Greg Fenwick, I am Mr. and Mrs. Olsen's personal assistant. They have agreed to see you, but I must ask you to keep it as brief as you can, as their time is *very* . . ."

Dehan had been sighing. Now she said, "Which office are they in, Greg?"

He licked his lips, turned, and made for May Olsen's door like he had the vestiges of his dignity clenched between his buttocks. He tapped, paused as though receiving telepathic instructions, and then pushed open the door.

"Detectives Stone and Dehan, from New York."

He stood back, and we entered before the Presence.

The office was large, larger than you would expect for a human rights lawyer unless she took on the White House most working days and counted Greenpeace and Abdul Rahman Yasin among her client list.

The left-hand wall was a concertina walnut panel, which I figured connected with Geoffrey's office on the other side. The right-hand wall was made up of two large windows with views of leafy D Street. Her desk was heavy oak and looked like a genuine antique, most of the wall space was taken up with mahogany bookcases, and the center of the floor was occupied by a solid, expensive coffee table, a suede sofa, and a couple of heavy armchairs. They were not a set. They were eclectic.

May was sitting behind the desk. The man I took to be Geoffrey, her husband, was perched on the corner of that desk, with one gleaming shoe placed on a leather chair. He looked relaxed and debonair in a beautifully tailored gray suit, and they were both looking at us, watching us.

My first impression of Geoffrey was that he was amiable and smart. He had an agreeable smile that masked a lack of moral backbone. But when I looked at her, my first impression was of her startling blue eyes. I found myself fumbling for a word to describe them, wound up with "uninhibited" and wondered why.

The door closed behind us, and May Olsen spoke.

"Detectives, you have made a considerable effort to ensure you saw us today, and I can't help but wonder what has two New York cops so keen to see a couple of humble immigration lawyers in Washington." Before we could answer, she gestured at the nest of chairs and the sofa and added, "Please, do sit and make yourselves comfortable. Can I offer you anything?"

Dehan sat on the suede sofa, and I shifted the angle of one of the armchairs so that I didn't have to turn my head to look at her. Before I sat I said, "No, thank you. Just so there is no confusion, I am Detective John Stone, this is Detective Carmen Dehan, we are both from the Forty-Third Precinct of the New York Police Department. Clearly we are outside our jurisdiction, and we are here only in a semiofficial capacity."

Geoffrey smiled and gave a little cough.

"What is a semiofficial capacity, Detective Stone? I don't recall that from law school."

"We were called to a crime scene last night. It was a homicide. There was a shallow grave in a cellar with a body in it. The grave appears to be between thirty and forty years old. The body has not as yet been identified. Beside the grave, also dead, was a woman in her thirties. She'd been shot in the chest. We believe her to be your daughter, April Olsen."

There was a moment of absolute silence. Geoffrey swallowed once, started to say something, shook his head and blinked, then said, "No."

May remained motionless for a few seconds, then sank back in her chair, and her face seemed to fold in on itself. Her features, attractive and elegant, became ugly and twisted, writhing on a spike of pain that could never be removed. Tears bathed her cheeks; her eyes and her nose swelled and became red. Then came the convulsive sobs, and she covered her face with her hands.

Geoffrey stood. His face was flushed. He turned to his wife, shaking his head. "No, May, this is ridiculous. There is some mistake. I spoke to her just . . ." Then his face began to go too. He raised both hands toward his face, and his eyes flooded. "I spoke to her . . . She was . . ." He sank into the chair that had moments before held his foot.

I said, "I am so sorry," and meant it. I made to stand and added, "We can come back some other time. We don't want to intrude."

May removed her hands from her face and took a couple of shuddering breaths. I stood and crossed the floor to her with my handkerchief in my hand. She took it, dabbed her eyes, and blew her nose. When she was done she said:

"No, you can't leave. You have to stay. We want to know. Geoffrey . . ." This last was addressed to her husband, who was bent double, with his elbows pressed into his belly, repeating over and over, "Oh God . . . Oh God . . . Oh God . . ."

She observed him a moment with dispassionate eyes. "Get a grip, old friend. We'll mourn her together later. You have to be strong now."

He looked up at her, with his mouth sagging open.

"How? I can't believe it. It's not true . . ."

She pressed a button on her desk, and after a moment the door opened and Greg looked in. His brow furrowed as he took in the scene. May didn't wait for him to ask.

"Take Geoffrey next door. Give him a stiff brandy. Comfort him. We have had some very bad news. We are not to be disturbed, you understand?"

He nodded, scowled at me and Dehan, and said, "Yes, Mrs. Olsen." Then he crossed the room, helped Geoffrey to his feet, and guided him out of the room.

After the door had closed, the room became deathly quiet for a moment. Dehan sat watching May Olsen. I stood in the middle of the floor, looking down at her as she sat, hunched, broken, breathing steadily, fighting the spasms of grief that must have been ravaging her inside.

Finally she got to her feet and came around the desk, where she sat in one of the armchairs. I took the other.

"So," she said, "what happened?"

"A neighbor heard a lot of activity, late at night, in the small hours. His cat couldn't sleep and kept him up. Eventually he got up and went to the window. There he saw all the lights on in his neighbor's house. Then he heard gunshots and called 911. We arrived and found what I described to you earlier."

"And you have no idea who the dead man was, what she was doing there, or who killed her?"

"None whatsoever. In fact, I was hoping you might be able to shed some light on it for us."

"I? Why? How could I possibly do that?"

"Well, for a start, the house was hers. Maybe you could tell us why she bought it."

FIVE

She was quiet for a long while. Then she stood and went to her desk, pulled open a drawer, and extracted a bottle of Johnnie Walker Black Label and a cut crystal tumbler. She gave us a hesitant look.

"You said you were semiofficial..."

I shook my head. "No, thanks. You go ahead."

She poured a generous measure and spilled a little in the process. She took a hungry pull and made her way back to the chair.

"You say she owned the house?"

Dehan asked her, "Did you not know that?"

"Where? Where was the house." She screwed her eyes shut. "Forty-Third Precinct, I don't know where that is. Bronx?"

Dehan said, "Yeah, the Bronx."

Her eyes came open and she stared at Dehan. "What part of the Bronx?"

I said, "Castle Hill," and watched her. She watched me back with glazed eyes. "Just south of Lafayette, Virgil Place."

Her eyes slipped from mine to stare at the carpet.

"Virgil Place?" She said it like she was speaking the deepest Congo. "What on Earth was she doing there?"

"That is something we hoped you would be able to help us with. You didn't know she had bought the house there?"

She frowned hard. "But she didn't live in the Bronx. She had an apartment here, in Washington. She had a profitable practice . . ."

Dehan said, "We'll need her address. What kind of practice?"

"She was an attorney. She specialized in international trade. She made a lot of money, and she was a little cynical about human and constitutional rights."

"Are you aware of any friends she had in New York, any connections, anything at all that would link her with the city?"

"No, I mean . . ." She sighed and gave a shrug that reeked of hopelessness. "We're . . . we're not that close. To be perfectly honest, as soon as she hit her teens, fifteen, she began to distance herself from us. She didn't approve of . . ."

We waited. After a moment I said, "Mrs. Olsen, we are homicide detectives and we specialize in cold cases, in the Bronx. That's why we are here. I have seen a lot of human rights outfits in my time, also in the Bronx, and they didn't look like this. I don't know what angle you have on human rights abuses, refugees, and immigration, but it clearly isn't the one that gets you a melamine desk in a back room with a secondhand computer and a green steel filing cabinet. Your operation may be legit or it may not, but that does not concern us. What does concern us is what had April in that house on Virgil Place."

She gave her head a small shake. "That's what I am trying to tell you. She decided when she was sixteen that she didn't approve of the way we approached human rights issues. She accused us of exploiting weak and vulnerable people for our own gain, yadda yadda. You know the way sixteen-year-olds carry on. I was probably just as obnoxious when I was a teenager. In fact I know I was. But she never quite seemed to grow up. We drifted apart."

Dehan grunted. "Okay, so she didn't tell you she'd bought the place in New York. How about the address on Virgil Place, does that mean anything to you? Did she ever mention it, or any people who might have lived there?"

"No. It means nothing to me, I'm afraid. I wish I could help, I really do."

"How about the name Marie Braun, or simply the surname Braun? Does that mean anything to you?"

Again she shook her head and frowned. "No, why? Who is Marie Braun?"

I said, "She's the woman April bought the house from. How about Allan Bernstein?"

A flicker of a smile, amusement. "Seriously? What has he to do with this? Of course I know Allan Bernstein. Anyone who was at Columbia at that time knew Allan Bernstein. He was notorious."

"Really? What can you tell us about him?"

"Not a lot. What anyone will tell you. I mean, he was a professor in the psychology department and I was an undergraduate in law, so what I heard was mainly gossip. But basically he was a fraud with a Carlos Castaneda fixation. He was always going on about altering consciousness and mind-expanding drugs, but really it was just a big front so he could have wild parties and screw his students."

Dehan said, "Do you know where those parties took place?"

She shook her head more emphatically. "Oh, no! I acquired two things at Columbia, apart from my degree: a level head and my husband. No, I had no desire to get involved with Allan and his gang of sixties nostalgia wannabes. He was an amusing figure to have in the background, and by all accounts he was a good writer and a good poet too, and highly intelligent. But that kind of scene was definitely not what I was looking for."

"What about your husband, Mrs. Olsen?"

"What about him? He had no contact with Bernstein either. He is in no state right now to answer questions, I'm afraid. I will hold it together until I get home. He hasn't got that kind of mettle. He is strong in a different way."

I said, "We will need to talk to him eventually."

"Of course you will. We'll arrange a FaceTime, or we'll go up to New York to meet with you. But not today."

She took another hefty pull on her whiskey. Her hand hadn't steadied any.

"Have you any other children, Mrs. Olsen?"

"Yes, April has a brother. Excuse me, April had a brother. It's hard to come to terms with . . ."

She bit her lip, and suddenly her eyes flooded and her nose was red. She spoke through wet lips, dabbing at them with my handkerchief. "It's so hard to believe . . ."

She squeezed her eyes shut, took a deep, ragged breath, and opened them again.

"Simon," she said. "His name is Simon. I should call him."

"Were they close?"

Her gaze was lost in a space a couple of feet in front of her. After a moment she said, "No, not really." She smiled and dropped her eyes, like she was smiling at some private joke. "He is more like his father, grounded, sensible, cautious, very family oriented." She listed the adjectives like she was reading them in a dream. "April was more like me. A bit of a rebel when there was a cause, a little uncompromising. Maybe that's the key word. Geoffrey and Simon will always compromise. Me and April—" She raised her face and smiled at me with her very blue eyes. "We'd ask you to spell it out for us. So, that's a long, roundabout way of saying that she wasn't close with me, or her father, or her brother."

Dehan was frowning. "They never used to meet, have lunch, visit . . . ?"

"You'd have to ask him."

I looked at Dehan. She gave her head a small shake. I drew breath to thank May Olsen and ask if we could come back some other time. But before I could speak, May gave a small, dry laugh.

"You don't know me, Detectives, so you are making an understandable mistake. We all have to experience pain in this world.

There is no opt-out clause. Buddha said it: pain is inevitable. But that doesn't mean you have to lie down and take it. Somebody killed my little girl, and I want to know who. I'll lick my wounds tonight, but right now we are going to sit down and work through this until we get some idea of why she bought that house."

She pulled her cell from her inside jacket pocket and pressed a speed-dial number. While it was ringing she said, "She didn't let it? Rent rooms to students? Get some kind of income from it?"

Dehan answered. "No, according to her neighbor, she would show up occasionally, stay a day or so, and then leave. Aside from that, it looked like it had remained untouched for years."

I added, "Perhaps decades."

She held my eye a moment then frowned.

"Simon? It's Mommy. Listen, we've had some bad news. I need you to drop whatever you're doing and come over to the office." She listened a moment, closed her eyes, and shook her head. "No, Simon, don't argue with me now. Just do as I say. Drop whatever it is and come straight here . . . I'll tell you when you get here."

She hung up and sat looking at the phone with her brow slightly creased, like she wasn't sure how she wound up with a phone in her hand.

"Speaking of decades," she said suddenly, "why did you ask me about Allan Bernstein?" Now she looked up at me. "What's he got to do with all this? The last I heard about him he had disappeared to Mexico to take peyote and screw Mexican girls." She glanced at Dehan and gave a tired, one-sided smile. "Sorry. That was insensitive."

Dehan shrugged. "Before that he was in New Mexico screwing New Mexican girls, and before that he was in New York screwing New Yorker girls. I'm not sensitive."

"Good for you. So what has he to do with my daughter's murder?"

I watched her carefully as I spoke. "The house where she was found, beside the grave of that other body, in the cellar, the house your daughter had bought from Mrs. Marie Braun, that house had originally belonged to Allan Bernstein."

She frowned hard. "Let me see if I understand you. Allan had a house, he sold it however long ago, to Marie Braun, who later sold it to my daughter, and you think that means Allan is connected to her murder? Isn't that overreaching a little, Detective? It's not even a coincidence. There must be tens of thousands of people in New York who were at Columbia during his tenure. Any number of them might have had children who bought his house. I just don't see what you're getting at."

I smiled in a way I thought was amiable.

"Well, I'm not actually getting at anything, Mrs. Olsen. But the link is not quite as tenuous as it seems. You see, Marie Braun was Bernstein's ex-wife. She didn't buy it from him. She inherited it from him when she had him declared dead."

She hesitated a moment. "His wife?"

"When Allan went to Mexico, she lost touch with him. After a few years she had him declared dead and inherited the house. A few years after that your daughter bought the house and did nothing with it—and I do mean *nothing*—save stay in it from time to time. From what my partner and I saw, she didn't even clean the place. All Allan's records, books, his record player . . . They were all there still. She barely touched it.

"Then, late last night, there was a lot of commotion. Apparently there were at least two people in the house. Shots were fired, and the cops who arrived on the scene found her in the basement. So, you see, even though there is no clear, causal link, nor a clear thread of connected events, there is a . . ." I paused, searching for the word. "A *continuity* about it that is striking."

She screwed up her eyes. "What are you suggesting, that my daughter was somehow involved with Allan Bernstein? That's absurd."

Dehan raised an eyebrow. "Is it? I guess that depends on what you mean by involved. Because the fact is that she is, actually, involved with Allan Bernstein. The question is, how far does that involvement go?"

May Olsen sighed and covered her face with her hands. She sat like that for a moment before dropping her hands into her lap.

"Look, Detectives, I don't know what point you are trying to make or what you are driving at. All I can tell you is that Allan Bernstein was a professor at Columbia when I was there back in the eighties. The gossip was that he went to Mexico. That would have been . . . eighty-six? Eighty-five or eighty-six. That is all I can tell you about him. I know nothing about his wife, this is the first I have heard about April having bought his house, and to the best of my knowledge there is absolutely no connection between April and Allan."

We were quiet for a moment, and she raised her eyes to meet mine.

"If I knew, if I had any information at all that could explain what my daughter was doing there, in that house, don't you think I would tell you?"

I nodded slowly a couple of times. "I would want to believe so. But I would also want to believe that people were incapable of murder, that husbands, wives, mothers, fathers, and sons and daughters were all incapable of hurting each other, of killing each other. Unfortunately, the people most likely to hurt us and kill us are the ones who love us the most. That's why courts deal in evidence and not assumptions, and why the burden of proof is so high. Somebody murdered your daughter, and someone concealed that other body under the concrete in Allan Bernstein's cellar. We are not going to find out who by assuming that people don't do that kind of thing."

She sagged back in her chair, flopped her head back, and closed her eyes.

"You're right, of course. I'm sorry." She opened her eyes, and her head came forward again. "It was a stupid thing to say. But the fact remains, I have absolutely no idea what she was doing there, or why she bought his house."

Outside we heard heavy footsteps on the stairs, and after a moment the door burst open and a man in his early thirties stepped in. He took in the scene at a glance and snapped, "What the *hell* is going on here?"

His mother stood and went to him. He put his arms around her as she spoke.

"Simon, these are police detectives from New York..."

"What are you doing in Washington? Let me see your credentials!"

I exchanged a glance with Dehan and we stood, pulling our badges. But May Olsen was shaking her head.

"Simon, listen to me. Detective Stone and Detective Dehan have brought some news. You need to sit and calm down and listen to them."

"Where is Daddy?"

"He's next door. He'll join us when he's feeling a little better. Now please, listen to what they have to tell you."

He sat slowly on the sofa, holding his mother. He fixed me with angry eyes.

"You had better have a damned good reason for this."

"Pipe down, Simon." It was Dehan. "A good reason for what? Keep mouthing off like that and you're going to feel pretty damn stupid when we tell you why we're here."

There wasn't a lot he could say to that, so his mouth worked a few times, and finally he said, "Well, why *are* you here?"

I'd had about as much of Simon Olsen as I was prepared to stomach. He wanted to play hardball, so I obliged.

"To inform you and your family that your sister was murdered in the small hours of last night. Now if you think that informing your mother of that fact is a breach of her civil rights, and attempting to investigate your sister's murder is a travesty against your family, we can just pack up, go back to New York, and let the case go cold. Is that what you want us to do?"

His blustering face had gone bright red. His mouth worked like a goldfish for a moment, and then the tears flooded his eyes.

"No," he said, "no, of course not, I'm sorry." And after a moment, "April, I, last night? I . . . how . . ." He turned to his mother as though he had only just realized she was there. "Mommy! You poor . . . It must have been such a shock! I am so sorry!"

They gripped each other, and he sobbed violently into her shoulder while she comforted him and stroked his hair.

"Not Appy," he said. "No, Mommy, not Appy!"

SIX

"I don't know if I can make you people understand." His eyes were wide, staring. "What you're talking about, what you're saying. It doesn't make any sense! It's . . ." He said "it's" again, three or four times in rapid succession. "It's not *real*! And you're asking me questions about *what*? About *who*? Allan *Bernstein*? What is he, some kind of *Jew*?"

"Baby!" May held his arm and stroked it, frowning reproachfully. "You don't mean that."

"I'm sorry, but *Bernstein*? Allan *Bernstein*? Who the hell is Allan *Bernstein*? And what the hell has he got to do with Appy?"

I paused a second for thought, then put my hands on my knees to rise.

"Mr. Olsen, you are clearly very upset and in no shape to be answering questions from the likes of us. Would you be willing to come to the precinct tomorrow, when you've had . . ."

"*Tomorrow?* Don't you people have any kind of human feelings?"

Dehan snarled, "Yeah, Simon! That's why we want to catch the bastard who murdered your sister! So her mother and father, and her brother, can have *some* measure of closure, if nothing else."

He closed his eyes. "I'm sorry . . ." He swallowed and said, "I'm sorry," again. "You don't know what it's like . . ."

"How do you know, wise guy? As a matter of fact I do. Both my parents were murdered right in front of me when I was a kid. And that wasn't the worst thing that happened that day. So quit bellyaching. For your information, your mother and your father just lost a daughter, and they could use the support of their son!"

He closed his eyes again. Obviously having his eyes open was not the big thing with Simon Olsen.

"My God!" he said after a moment, "I am such an egotist. Mommy, I am so sorry. This must be hell for you. I am so selfish. Please forgive me. I'll try to be strong for . . ."

I couldn't take much more, so I stood.

"Mr. Olsen, we can either do this now, or you can come and talk to us at the Forty-Third. Either way we are going to need one of you to identify her. But this conversation is one we need to have, sooner rather than later."

"Yes, of course. I am so sorry, my behavior has been . . . please forgive me. This has been . . ."

"Can we expect you tomorrow, at the station?"

"I'll be there, after lunch. I'll call you when I'm on my way."

Dehan stood.

"Will you identify April?"

Simon glanced at his mother, and she stood.

"I'll come with him. I'll identify her. She is my daughter. I'd like to say goodbye."

I tried not to look at Simon, whose face had screwed up into a sobbing ball again. We moved for the door, and Simon, wiping his face with a handkerchief, reached for the handle to open it.

"The house," he said. "The house on Virgil Place, I remember she bought that. I remember her buying it."

I paused in the doorway, looking down at him.

"She discussed it with you?"

"Yes."

"When?"

"Oh, way back when she bought it, ninety-something."

May was frowning at him. "Why didn't you tell me, Si?"

"I . . . she asked me not to."

"Why?" There was an edge to her voice. "Why would she do that?"

I cut in before they could get a conversation going.

"What I would really like to know, Mr. Olsen, is what made her buy that house in the first place. Why that house in particular?"

He nodded and ran his big hands through his hair. "I'll give it some thought. I think I am probably going to be of very little use to you right now, Detective. I can't think straight. But I will think about your question."

"Yeah, I'd also like you to think about whether she ever spoke to you about Allan Bernstein, or any of his pupils. We'll expect you tomorrow at lunchtime."

"Yes." He nodded. "Of course." He wiped his face with big, blond hands. His nails were meticulously manicured. Then he ran his fingers through his hair.

"I don't recall anything about that offhand, but as I say, I'll give it some thought."

Dehan gave a single nod and moved to pass through the door. Then she looked back at him. "You were obviously very close."

He shrugged, like he thought her question was a stupid one.

"She was my sister."

"You get all kinds of brothers and sisters. You get all kinds of family. Some are close, some aren't. It looks like you were close to your sister."

He took hold of the door to close it.

"I guess," he said, then, "Please, Detectives, we are very shaken and unsettled, and we need some time alone. I will talk to you tomorrow."

She nodded. "Sure. We'll see you tomorrow."

We left the building, out into the afternoon sunshine, climbed into the car, and pulled away in silence. I drove north on

13th Street, across Maryland Avenue, as far as H Street. There I turned right and east and parked opposite the Ella Grace.

Dehan looked at me and said, "What's this?"

"I need to think."

We climbed out, crossed the road, and pushed into the cool, redbrick quiet of the bar. I ordered two ice-cold beers, and we found a small, round table by the window with a couple of bentwood chairs. I handed Dehan her beer and sat.

I pulled off half my drink, and Dehan sat and wagged a long, slender index finger at me.

"She is a powerful woman. She chose a husband she could control and gave birth to a chinless wonder who, or whom, she brought up to be obedient to and dependent on 'Mommy.' Her daughter was like her and was having none of it, so she split. None of this, Stone, points to any involvement in homicide."

I grunted and pulled off half of the remaining half, smacked my lips, and sucked my teeth.

"I know what you're thinking," she said, and reached for her beer, then flopped back in her chair without taking hold of it. "You're thinking it's a weird family and just the kind of breeding ground where your Freudian neurotics become Freudian psychotics and wind up killing each other. But you're wrong."

"That's not what I am thinking."

"It's not?"

"No, I'm thinking that if you don't do something about your beer soon, I will."

She picked up her glass, took a sip, and left a creamy white moustache. "Happy? I'm telling you I think you're on the wrong scent."

"I haven't said a word about my scent yet." I was about to add that she had a moustache but decided not to. "I confess, Dehan, that I am at a complete loss. This case definitely has what Holmes would have called 'interesting features.' Right now, I am stumped. What are your thoughts? You tell me. I can tell you have some."

She nodded. "I have." She took another, longer pull on the

beer and leaned back in her chair, cradling the beer over her belly. "Okay, this is my theory. It is not yet a hypothesis," she said, and smirked.

"Good Lord, Dehan. I love it when you talk like that. I go all weak at the knees."

"The guy in the shallow grave is definitely not Bernstein."

"What makes you so sure?"

"Wait. Don't interrupt. Bernstein left suddenly for New Mexico, and then Mexico. This is a very successful academic with a good future who is having a ball. The kind of ball academics have not enjoyed in this country since Tim Leary tuned in, dropped out, and turned on."

"Turned on, tuned in, and dropped out."

"Whatever. The fact is, he was having a ball. And a guy in that position, enjoying the security and the status of a professor at Columbia University, does not just drop everything and go. He has to have a very good reason."

"And what is the reason?"

"Like we discussed before. He killed somebody and went on the lam."

"Sometimes you talk like Mickey Spillane."

"I love Mickey Spillane. The body in the basement is somebody Bernstein killed while he was out of his mind on some mind-altering drug, and he escaped to Mexico like thousands of killers before him. It is the simple explanation. *Entia non sunt* and all that jazz."

I shrugged. "Okay, it has the advantage of providing a simple explanation for one of the bodies and the disappearance of Bernstein across the border to Mexico. But it goes absolutely no way toward explaining why April Olsen bought the house, or why she was shot to death standing beside that open grave."

She drew breath, opened her mouth, and clamped it shut again.

"No," she said finally. "But I don't want to get drawn into some tortuous Chinese puzzle where nothing fits and nothing is what it seems, pursuing motives and relationships that don't exist and never did."

I sighed. "See? You take the fun out of everything."

"And if we start imagining weird connections, I don't know, like April became obsessed with Bernstein and his ideas. Tracked him down and started corresponding with him. She fell in love, and they entered into a relationship . . ."

"He is now seventy-five or eighty."

"Yeah, but he's probably living barefoot in some desert hacienda eating macrobiotic food and doing asanas to the sun every morning over porridge and green tea. Some girls go for wise old men. What can I tell you?"

I raised a severe eyebrow at her. "I am neither wise nor old. I am mature and foolish."

"Whatever. That kind of scenario . . ."

"Which I happen to think is very plausible."

"Yeah, it kind of is, but if we go down that path, we are going to drive ourselves nuts and we will never close the case. It is not anything weird like that. He killed a guy while he was high and he ran to Mexico, in time-honored fashion." She poked at me in the air several times. "And you, you are going to try to make it weird."

I smiled. "I promise not to try to make it weird. But going back to your interesting theory that April became fascinated with this latter-day Timothy Leary, tracked him down, and became infatuated with him. This would explain why she bought the house and left it as it had been when he was there. It might also explain her occasional retreats to the house. But how does it lead us to her standing over this man's grave and getting shot?"

She took another swig of her beer and wiped the froth from her lips with the back of her wrist.

"If I were you, wanting to overcomplicate things, I'd say that back in eighty-five or thereabout, Bernstein had had the concrete lifted from his basement because he was planning to grow weed down there, or poppies or ayahuasca or some crazy shit like that. At one of his crazy parties he was showing a friend the preparations he had made. They got into a row over something, it doesn't matter what because they were out of their minds, Bernstein suddenly metamorphosed into Oedipus, high on acid, he believed the other guy was his father, and shot him, or more likely stabbed him with a sword, for phallic effect.

"Next morning, realizing what he had done, and with an almighty hangover, he buried his friend, told everyone he was going to Mexico to experiment with peyote, and fled the country.

"Now, thirty-odd years later, April Olsen tracks him down. How did she become interested in him? That's easy, both her parents were at Columbia, both must have had stories, and not only that, two gets you twenty May and Geoffrey have friends from back in the day who also remember crazy Dr. Bernstein and his wild parties. These stories appealed to her, and she started researching him. Eventually she tracked him down to his adobe hut. She was seduced by the fact that he was now so exotic and wise, and he was seduced by the fact that she was young and beautiful and smelt of expensive toiletries instead of goat manure. She tells him she has bought his house and conserved it exactly as it was, and he starts to feel nostalgic. He wants to come home."

"But?"

"But here is a missing piece. Something makes her suspicious. Now that she has met him, she can't understand why he would just drop everything and go and live in an adobe hut. She begins to suspect something is amiss. Perhaps she finds some clues . . ."

"What kind of clues?"

"Old receipts for cement, spades, a pickaxe. Stuff that would suggest work had been done in the cellar. You saw the house. Nothing had been touched since the day he left. So she decides she has to dig up the cellar floor. She does, not that night, the night before. And he is due to arrive that night—last night. He does, and that's the car Garner heard. And she is all gorgeous because . . ." She leaned forward and pointed at me. "She doesn't care that he's a killer. It just makes him more fascinating. So she is dressed for dinner, looking gorgeous for him. And she takes him down to the cellar to show him what she has found, and swear eternal fidelity to him, because dames are stupid like that sometimes..."

"Good to know. Thanks for the heads-up."

"He takes one look at what she's done and he blows her away. He can't have witnesses. He turns around and goes straight back to Mexico."

"That's not a bad theory, Dehan. It's crazy enough to be true."

"Yeah, I wound up kind of half convincing myself."

"So, if April was able to trace Bernstein to Mexico, we should be able to do so too. Where do you suppose she started?"

She thrust out her lower lip and picked up her glass again.

"His colleagues at work. People who knew him at the university. That's the obvious starting point. Which reminds me they should be contacting us soon. And while we're at it, we should ask if anybody else has been asking questions about him."

"In the last few years."

"Yeah."

I drummed my fingers on the table. "It's good. We also need to get DNA samples from Marie Braun's kids and compare them with the body in the grave." I shrugged and smiled. "You never know, we might get lucky and he'll ping on CODIS in five minutes because his name is Toni Bonebreaker Corleone. On the other hand he might not be on CODIS at all and then we will have to establish who he is. Obviously the first person to eliminate will be Bernstein."

"Obviously. It's his house, he disappeared, it could be his body. So if we don't hear from the Braun kids by tonight, we need to go after the nursing home and compel them to give us the contact details."

"We also need to ask the Mexican authorities to issue a BOLO for Bernstein. It's a forlorn hope, he could be anywhere—he could be dead. But we can ask anyhow."

She shrugged. "Not so forlorn, perhaps. A guy like Bernstein could have been in and out of Mexican jails a few times over the last thirty-odd years. He may well be in their system."

"It's worth a try. Okay, you done?"

She nodded, drained her glass, and stood. In that moment my phone rang.

"Stone."

"Detective Stone, this is Phil Herman, at Columbia. I kind of run things in the Psychology and Social Sciences Department. I got a message you wanted to talk about a professor we had here back in the dawn of time . . ."

SEVEN

I was sitting with my ass on the hood above the wheel of the old Mark II, and Dehan was leaning on the burgundy roof, with her chin on her forearms, watching me and listening. The sun was turning copper, and the shadows of gabled roofs and chimney pots were lying long across the bronze blacktop of H Street.

I had the phone on speaker and I was saying, "It was a long time ago, Professor Herman. How well did you know him?"

He gave a small laugh. "I caught the tail end of the Bernstein era. I was just assistant professor back then. I didn't know him well, personally. I attended one of his famous parties, but that was quite enough for me. Shortly after that he decamped to Mexico, and that was the end of that. May I ask why you are interested in him?"

"Yeah, but I would rather not discuss it over the phone. Can you put me in touch with anyone who actually knew him well at the time?"

"Sure, there are a couple of people around here who have become ossified in their jobs. Most of them are semiretired, but you know how it is in universities. They hang around the corridors, looking like intellectuals and pretending to smoke pipes, trying to be acceptably controversial . . ." He broke off to roar with laughter, fitting neatly into his own caricature as he did so. "Nobody is actually sure if they still work here, but they have become venerable and nobody wants to tell them to go away either. I can gather a couple of them up for you, but what do you want me to do with them? What shall I tell them?"

"I just want to meet with them—you too, Dr. Herman, if you're available—so that you can give us some background on Allan Bernstein."

"Um . . . *why*? How can Allan Bernstein possibly be of interest to anybody anymore, Detective?"

"Forgive me, Professor, but like I said. It's something I am not going to discuss on the phone. Can you arrange it?"

"Of course, come to my office on the campus tomorrow, say eleven a.m.? Perhaps you can enlighten us and we can enlighten you."

I let a smile tinge my voice. "I'm sure Professor Bernstein would approve."

There was a pause, an unamused laugh, and, "Yes, quite. I'll see you tomorrow, then."

I hung up, and Dehan's chin was still on her forearms so talking made her whole head move.

"Maybe they'll have photographs."

I nodded. "Though I am not sure how recognizable his face is right now."

She stood erect and banged softly with her palm on the roof of the car a couple of times.

"Okay, big guy, let's make a move."

By the time we finally got back to the Bronx it was just after nine p.m. Frank had called when we were on the way and said they'd be working late if we wanted to pass by the lab. When we got there, Joe was with him. They were sitting in the small nook Frank called his office drinking black coffee laced with whiskey.

Frank stood as we went in.

"Why are you two out at this time of night? My wife tells me married couples should be at home, together, when the sky turns dark."

"She's right, but that's for nice people, not cops and MEs. We come out when it gets dark, and practice our black arts."

Frank shook his head at Joe. "My God! It has a literary bent! How grotesque is that?"

Dehan yawned elaborately. "Not that this ain't fun, boys, but it's been a long day. Is this a social visit, or have you got something?"

Joe frowned at Frank. "Am I making this up, or did she used to be nice?"

"I was never nice, Joe. If anything I was worse. Now, with that sorted out, what have we got?"

He raised his plastic cup. "Coffee and Johnnie Walker."

"Funny."

"Fine! First, GPR revealed nothing. Second, her name was April Olsen, as you suspected. Her prints were in the system for driving under the influence of alcohol. She had also been arrested for possession of cannabis and cocaine. She claimed it had been planted on her, nothing could be proved, so the prosecution was dropped. The prints and DNA on the toothpaste and the brush, and all over the bathroom, were hers."

Frank took over. "She was shot twice through the chest at pretty much point-blank range. One shot penetrated the heart on the left side—her left side. The other went high and tore her trachea and her windpipe in half. The fact that at such close range, both bullets didn't find the heart . . ."

Dehan interrupted, "Shooter isn't used to using a gun."

"That is what I was going to say, but you said it so much better. Death was instantaneous."

Joe said, "As you know, there was no weapon at the scene of the crime, and there were no casings. However, two slugs were recovered. Both .45 cal. Not so common these days. Joe is having them analyzed."

I said, "So he may have been using a revolver."

"The absence of casings suggests a revolver, and statistically a nine-millimeter tends to be a semiautomatic these days. Revolvers are not so popular anymore, probably for their limited magazine capacity and their weight. But the fact is they leave less evidence behind."

I nodded. "Anything else?"

Frank glanced at Joe. "Yeah. She had cement dust under her toenails and her fingernails. There were also small granules of it ingrained in her hands and her feet."

Dehan frowned. "What does that mean?"

Frank spread his hands. "Beats me. You saw her. She was dressed up nice. She had showered, she had exotic oils on her skin and in her hair . . ."

I said, "She looked like she was going on a date."

It was Dehan who answered. "Not necessarily. Guys just shower. Some women put on all kinds of oils and stuff just to feel good."

I grunted, and Frank went on. "But I think you're kind of missing the point. She had showered and made herself up, but she still had cement particles in her toenails and her fingernails, and encrusted in her palms and the soles of her feet . . ."

"No, I get it," I said. "She'd been digging, and the particles . . ."

"Minute particles—"

". . . were so encrusted they hadn't come out in the shower."

"That's the interpretation I put on it. I'm talking about minute particles. She thought she was clean, but she wasn't. And that means she had done a lot of digging. Hours."

Dehan scowled and scratched her head, leaning on the doorjamb.

"So, you're saying she dug up the body?"

Joe shook his head. "No, not at all. That is too big a leap. What he is saying is that she had cement dust in her shoes..."

"The red ones she was wearing that night?"

"No, other shoes we did not find at the scene. So she had cement dust in her shoes or her boots or whatever, and as she tramped around"—he made tramping motions with his feet—"the particles of dust got ground into her skin, especially the small folds you have on the soles of your feet. The same thing is evident on her hands. She was probably wearing gloves, though not necessarily, and whatever she was doing, it was hard work because the dust got into her clothes, and from there got ground into her nails and into her skin."

Dehan spread her hands wide, hunched her shoulders, and appealed to me with her face. "So she was digging!"

"Only if you are a normal human being, Dehan. If you are a forensic scientist, you were tramping around making a lot of effort in a hole."

Frank said, "Story of my life, my marriage, my job..."

I ignored his comment. "So this is consistent with her digging the hole, or at least getting into the hole and doing strenuous work there."

"Oh yes, oh certainly. And for a long while. It took a lot of effort to get those granules so well ingrained."

Dehan went away and came back with two ergonomic chairs on wheels. She shoved one at me and straddled the other.

"Any more of that coffee going? I am exhausted."

Joe found a couple of plastic cups and half filled them. He handed us one each and sat down again.

"I'm not a detective," he said. "At least, not your kind of detective. Me and Frank, we have to work by strict empirical rules of syllogistic deduction. But if I were a *cop* rather than a scientist, I would say—and please understand I am *not* saying this because I am *not* a cop—either she dug the hole or she got into the hole and did a lot of work in there."

Dehan stared at me quietly. "Son of a gun," she said at last.

Then she turned back to Joe and Frank, glancing at them each in turn. "What about the guy in the hole?"

"We've had no hits on his DNA. His fingers are very distorted, but we used the Walker rehydration technique, adapted from Ruffer, and by tomorrow we should be able to get some prints to run through the system."

I asked, "How did he die?"

"He was shot, twice, in the chest."

"Did you recover the slugs?"

"Yes, they were still lodged in his rib cage."

"And?"

"Both .45 cal, like the girl. Joe is running a comparison."

Dehan shook her head into her coffee. "Man, this is a total mind f . . ." She drank, stifling the word. When she'd swallowed she smacked her lips. "What does this mean? That the same person who shot him, thirty-five years ago, came back and shot her, in the same place, thirty-five years later? Why? It doesn't make any sense!"

Frank was shaking his head. "See? This is what Joe meant by being empirical and using syllogistic logic. The same *gun* may have been used—*may* have been used—in both killings. But it is an unwarranted leap to say from that that the same *person* was wielding the gun. In fact, the evidence suggests just the opposite."

I said, "The placing of the shots?"

Frank nodded. "Precisely. One of the shots fired at April went wide of the mark, which suggests somebody unfamiliar with guns. Whereas both of the shots fired at the man in the hole, as you call him, punctured the rib cage directly above the heart at about two millimeters from each other."

"Using a .45, that takes some control."

"And not just physical." It was Joe. "Killing a person is emotionally very intense. But this killer apparently didn't flinch, and was not shaken afterwards either. He remained very cool and fired twice in rapid succession without losing focus."

I looked at Dehan. "So we might be dealing with somebody

who is accustomed to using guns." I turned back to Joe and Frank. "Anything else, for now?"

Frank answered. "Not really. I need more time. I am dealing with a mummy after all. We don't get a lot of those in the Bronx. I can tell you he was in his forties, about six one, dark hair, and, judging by the size of his clothes and the setting of his belt buckle, on the heavy side. Aside from that, nada."

I nodded. "Tomorrow I am going to have some DNA brought to you from one of Professor Allan Bernstein's daughters. Can you determine from comparing the results whether the body is Allan Bernstein's?"

"To a high degree of probability, yes."

Joe frowned. "You think it's Bernstein?"

I thought about it. In the end I shook my head and sighed noisily.

"I don't think anything at the moment. If it's him, somebody killed him and I have no idea why. If it's not him, we have only conjecture. He seems to have fled to Mexico, that suggests..."

Frank nodded. "Conjecture." He shrugged. "Well, we'll try to have a bit more fact for you tomorrow. Meantime, try and get me that sample and we'll see if we can establish who he was."

I stood, and Dehan levered herself to her feet.

"Thanks for the coffee, boys."

We made our way down through the empty building and out into the parking lot, where soulless light gave a lonely yellow sheen to the few cars parked under the trees, and made our way toward the old burgundy bruiser. We were five minutes from home and my belly was telling me I needed a steak and a glass of wine. But Dehan leaned her forearms on the roof of the car and stood looking at me.

"You know what worries me?"

I unlocked the door. "That we'll never get home tonight and have dinner?"

She nodded. "Yeah, that too. But aside from that, if it is him."

"I know, but we've only had the case twenty-four hours,

Dehan, less in fact. The guy was a real character by the sounds of it, and wasn't afraid of upsetting people. It's not impossible he made somebody upset enough to pop him."

"I guess, a jealous boyfriend or something."

"That is not impossible." I spread my hands and leaned my forearms on the roof opposite her, dangling the keys from my fingers. "But it is equally possible that he popped the jealous boyfriend. What has me going is the fact that the same gun was used. That is very, very suggestive."

She nodded. "Yeah. Same weapon, different person." She gazed up into the dim, lamplit trees, where confused birds were still singing desultory songs. "Are we looking at a weapon passed down from father to son? Are we looking at revenge?"

I tapped the keys on the roof and made a "hmmm" noise. "How would that work?"

"Dad shoots Bernstein for screwing around with his wife. Body is never found, everybody believes he's gone to Mexico . . ." She faltered.

"What makes everybody believe he's gone to Mexico? And why did April buy the house? What was she doing down there that night, and previous nights, by the sound of it? We need to talk to the inspector and have him talk to Washington PD so we can go and search her apartment. We need to know a lot more about April Olsen. What was motivating her, what made her tick."

She sighed and sagged her head onto her arms. "We just haven't enough data. Enough for one night, Stone." She looked up and smiled. "You know what else is suggestive?"

I smiled back. "I hope you're going to tell me."

"When you said we would never get home for dinner. The way you said 'dinner,' like that. That was real suggestive."

I pulled open the door.

"Well you just wait, kiddo, till I start saying things like," I growled, "seared steak, succulent sirloin, oaked red wine, and fried potatoes. Then you'll really be in trouble."

She made a noise midway between a whimper and a sigh and climbed in beside me.

"Don't stop, goddamn it! Tell me more, you culinary beast! Tell me more!"

I laughed as I pulled out of the parking lot, telling her a morally reprehensible story about lamb cutlets and mint jelly.

It too was suggestive.

EIGHT

THE NEXT DAY AT 10:55 A.M. I PARKED ON AMSTERDAM Avenue, at the corner with West 119th, and we crossed the road to enter the campus beside the Department of Psychology. And ten minutes after that we were being admitted to a large room that was on the luxurious side of old-world grand. The walls were paneled in oak. A vast, highly polished mahogany table stood on a vast, burgundy Persian rug in the center of the floor, beneath a vast chandelier. Bookcases from floor to ceiling held books whose collective value was probably more than my house several times over, and here and there, there were Chesterfield chairs that looked old enough to have been sat in by George II, back when it was King's College.

The person doing the admitting was Professor Philip Herman. He was nothing like the image I had created in my mind, based on his voice. He was still youthful in his early sixties. He was dressed in Levi's and an expensive, linen shirt with no collar, open at the neck. He was bald on top, but the hair at the back and sides of his head reached down past his shoulders. On his feet he had leather boots that looked handmade. His smile was genial and a little mischievous.

"Detectives!" he said. "How nice that you are punctual. Please come in."

He stood with his arms extended into an expansive cross, using his right hand to shepherd us and his left to indicate where we should go, toward two chairs with their backs to us at the table.

There were two other men in the room. One was watching us from the comfort of a Chesterfield with what looked like a cup of tea resting in a china saucer in his hand. He was somewhere in the vicinity of seventy-five and had his scrawny body wrapped in a thousand-dollar dark blue pinstripe suit. There was absolutely no expression on his face.

The other guy was roughly the same age, but, though he was also bald on top, his hair was down to his waist, tied back in a ponytail. He had on a Hugo Boss cream linen jacket, matching chinos, and Nike trainers. Obviously a lifetime researching the human mind and human behavior at Columbia does not necessarily make you an original thinker when it comes to style.

Herman wanted to guide us toward the two chairs. I figured he had some obscure, psychological motivation so I made for the head of the table, and Dehan went for the other end.

Herman watched us and smiled, then pointed with his open hand at the guy in the Hugo Boss suit. "Professor Jay Petrov, runs the social psychoanalysis program, and"—gesturing at the scrawny guy who hadn't risen from his Chesterfield—"Professor Hal Mahoney, behavioral sciences. Both were close friends of Professor Bernstein." He stretched his arms out into a cross again, to gesture at both of us, and addressed Petrov and Mahoney. "Detectives Carmen Dehan and John Stone." He grinned. "I don't think I need to specify which is which. Shall we join them at the table?"

Mahoney sighed loudly and got to his feet. Petrov moved to the table and pulled out a chair to sit beside Dehan. Herman sat beside him on my right, and Mahoney came around and sat on my left. He cleared his throat and spoke.

"Let me make it very clear from the start that I will not be a party to any attempt to smear Allan's name or his contribution in the field of cognitive research and altered states of consciousness."

Dehan stared at him a moment, then looked at me and shrugged.

"That's swell," she said.

I looked around the table. "Anybody else got a statement to make?"

Petrov spoke to me while he smiled at Dehan.

"Can we dispense with you and get another one like Carmen?"

"No. Let's start with you, Jay." He didn't like that, and he turned to look at me with dilated nostrils. I smiled agreeably and went on. "How well did you know Professor Bernstein?"

"We were intimate friends for many years. We collaborated on research, and I helped him through the nightmare of his divorce."

Dehan said, "What does that mean, you helped him through his divorce? What did you do that was helpful, Jay?"

He sighed and flopped back in his chair. "He was a very brilliant man, largely underrated, because he was a social nonconformist who was highly critical of the established order. His thesis was that there was, indeed, a revolution in the years between 1967 to 1970, but that the establishment won the war and from that time on systematically crushed and repressed free thought and free expression."

"What has that got to do with his divorce?"

"I'm getting there, Carmen. Allan was a man who lived by his beliefs. And one of his core beliefs was that love was channeled through sex, sex elevated consciousness, and that sex and love should be free. 'Why don't we d-do it in the road?' Right? The Beatles. He didn't just preach that stuff, he lived by it in the decade dominated by Ronald Reagan and Margaret Thatcher, the decade of free-market greed and crass materialism. He was out there preaching free love and holding the wildest parties you ever went to in your life, baby. One night at his pad in the Bronx did more to free your mind than twenty years of meditation in the Himalayas. I'll tell you that for nothing." He nodded vigorously, laughing a humorless laugh. "And I have *been* to the Himalayas to meditate."

Dehan repressed a sigh. "Is that where his divorce lawyer was? Did you go to fetch him? I ask because I am still wondering what this has to do with his divorce and how you helped him."

Petrov groaned elaborately. "Okay, I thought you wanted to get an understanding of the man. Obviously that is too much to ask for. Marie, that was his wife, did not have what you would call exactly an open mind. Her mind was narrow *and* closed. When he started experimenting with hallucinogens, it *really* freaked her out. She was not happy. So pretty soon, me, Hal, and Allan would meet at his place to conduct experiments, and she would leave. You know? At first I tried to help her. I tried to persuade her to stay and join in, be a part of it and dig the scene, as Allan used to say. But she didn't want to know. She was sweet, cute, but in the end she went running to Mommy every time we had a session."

He shrugged. "So, when she was gone we started to relax more, chill more, started to get groovier results, and Allan said he wanted to include more people in the experiments, to see what kind of group consciousness we could develop. Some of those people who joined us were girls. One night Marie came back and found what *she* called an 'orgy'"—he made speech mark signs in the air with his fingers—"going on in her house. She packed her bags and left. Over the next few months he needed *a lot* of moral support to get through the barrage of narrow-minded materialism which the world threw at him."

I showed him my palm.

"Let me stop you there for a moment. There are a couple of things I am not clear about. First of all, these extra people who started joining in what you call your experiments, who were they? Were they Professor Bernstein's students?"

"By and large, yes."

Dehan snapped, "What does 'by and large' mean? Were they his students or not?"

He scowled at her. I wondered if he still wanted to swap me for another one like her. He said, "By and large means that mostly they were, but there might have been one or two who were not his students."

"Another thing," I went on, "I understood he had children. Where were they during all this fiasco?"

"He had two children, Rachel and Stella."

Mahoney drew breath and spoke suddenly.

"That was particularly tragic."

I turned to him and frowned. "It was tragic that he had two daughters?"

"That would be fatuous. Allow me to finish. It was tragic because he adored his eldest daughter, Rachel. But Stella was born some eight months or so after they separated. This was his parting gift to his wife. He gave her life, a beautiful daughter, whom he never got to know. Part of what made the divorce proceeding so very painful for our friend was the cruelty with which Marie attempted to ban him from having any contact with the children. She told the court that he was a dangerous madman who, through the abuse of psychedelic drugs, had become psychotic, and she feared for her own safety and that of her children."

Dehan was frowning at her pad, taking notes. I asked him, "Was he ever violent, Professor Mahoney?"

He made a scornful noise through his nose.

"That's ridiculous. His whole thesis was about love and peace. He was not a violent man."

There was something in his tone of voice that didn't convince me, and Dehan threw me a glance that said she had caught it too.

I turned to Petrov. "Would you agree with that, Jay?"

He was studying his hands on the tabletop. "Largely, yes."

Dehan spoke without looking up from her notes. "That's a qualified answer."

"Well done, Detective Dehan. Well spotted." His tone was dry.

She raised her eyes from her pad. "So what's stopping you from giving an unqualified answer?"

Mahoney scowled at his colleague. "Jay . . . ?"

"I can't lie, Hal, goddamn it! You know as well as I do that toward the end he started having tantrums, and some of those were pretty damned scary."

I said, "What do you mean by 'toward the end'?"

Petrov shook his head. "It's just an expression. Don't read too much into it. I mean before he went to Mexico. The stress of the divorce, pressure from the university to moderate his behavior and toe the line, the pain caused by his wife's attacks and the court's decision to deny him access to his children . . . It all began to have a cumulative effect, and he began to have violent outbursts."

Dehan spoke to the paper again as she wrote.

"Of course it had nothing to do with the vast quantities of hallucinogenic drugs and alcohol that he was consuming."

Professor Mahoney answered. "I am quite sure they had a lot to do with it too. But where his mind was opening and evolving, growing and developing in ways that we cannot imagine, because of the repressive control this government exercises over any kind of mental expansion, that growth and development was conditioned—*affected*—by all the cruelty and vitriol that was directed at him. He was a brilliant man with an extraordinary mind, breaking ground in research into what consciousness is, and what *identity* is. And all the world was able to see was a university professor abusing his position so he could take drugs and screw his students. Well, I'm afraid that says far more about his detractors than it says about him!"

"Yeah, that's very moving, Professor, but I'm afraid it doesn't answer my question, or tell me very much about these violent outbursts. What, precisely, do you mean by 'toward the end,' and what form did these violent outbursts take? What provoked them?"

Hal Mahoney slammed his open palm down on the table. It made a very small noise.

"This is *exactly* what I did not want to be a party to. This is *precisely* why I did not want to be a part of this. It is exactly what he predicted, that his name and his research would be dragged through..."

I'd had enough, and I interrupted him. "Professor, I don't know why you think you're here, and I am not really interested. But this has nothing to do with the establishment versus free thinkers. We are homicide cops, and we specialize in cold cases. We are investigating two murders that were committed at Professor Bernstein's address, and we need background, and we need to understand what happened thirty-five years ago in his house. Now if you have information which is relevant to this investigation, whether you like it or not, you are compelled by law to give it to us." He drew breath, and I cut him short. "What was the nature of Professor Bernstein's violent outbursts, and" —I turned to Jay Petrov—"what did you mean by 'toward the end'?"

It was Petrov who answered. "The combination of the various stresses that were being put on Allan, plus"—he nodded sarcastically at Dehan—"the extended use of drugs and alcohol, began to take its toll on him. He began to talk more and more about escaping from New York and finding some kind of lawless paradise where he could conduct his research free from the ignorance and prejudice of the system. That, when we talk about Allan, is what we refer to as the end. During that period he went three or four times..."

Mahoney cut in: "Three."

"Three times to New Mexico to experiment with peyote. Peyote does not grow naturally in New Mexico. The only state where it occurs naturally in the USA is Texas, in a narrow strip along the Rio Grande. But Allan didn't like the vibes in Texas. He used to say it wasn't cowboy country, it was pig-boy country. But he knew some people in New Mexico who cultivated it, some Mexicans. Don't ask me who they were because I have no idea. I never met them, and I never had the chance to go with him."

Mahoney took up the narrative.

"He spent more and more time down there, ignoring the threats from the university. He said he had found peace, and an environment where he could pursue his research unencumbered by what he called Western Institutional Stupidity. In the end he wrote to us, to me and to Jay, and told us that his Mexican friends had told him about a shaman in Mexico, somewhere in Sonora, and he was going to go there and meet him." He shrugged. "We never heard from him again."

Dehan asked, "He never wrote to you from Mexico?"

"I just told you that."

"You never tried to find him?"

They both stared hard at the tabletop and shook their heads. Petrov muttered, "No, we never did. And to be honest, he had become a liability to the university, and they were very happy to see the back of him. When Marie had him declared officially dead, the entire institution sighed a massive, collective sigh of relief."

"So that is the period you refer to as 'the end' or 'nearing the end'; what about these violent outbursts?"

Mahoney glanced over at Petrov. "You tell him. I don't want to."

Petrov spread his hands and shrugged.

"In the beginning it was nothing. If he heard from his lawyer, or from Marie, he would fly into a rage, break things, stuff like that. We thought nothing of it because he was always a very intense man. But gradually the attacks of fury became more frequent, and they were triggered ever more easily. He would take it out mainly on his students. Especially the girls."

Dehan asked, "Is there any particular girl who stood out? Whom he was especially close with?"

"Yeah, sexy little creature. She was as crazy as he was, and they really liked each other. What was her name, Hal?"

Mahoney sighed and shook his head. "I can't remember. It was a long time ago."

Petrov snapped his fingers. "Rose?"

Mahoney nodded. "Yeah, Rose. He used to call her his little Rosie. They were very close."

"She was a student?"

"Yeah."

"Surname? Photos?"

Herman spoke for the first time since we'd arrived. He said, "I can get someone on that and have a copy emailed or WhatsApped to you if we find anything."

I nodded at him. "I appreciate that." I turned back to Petrov and Mahoney. "How about any guys he was having trouble with? Any jealous boyfriends, husbands, anything like that?"

They both made faces at each other, shrugged, and shook their heads.

"No, nothing like that."

I looked across at Dehan. She gave her head a small shake. I said, "Okay, I think we are pretty much done for now. There is just one last thing. Has anybody else, either recently or further back in time, tried to trace Professor Bernstein in Mexico? Has anybody come asking questions about him, trying to find him?"

The three of them frowned at each other and nodded. It was Petrov who spoke: "Yeah, there was, but this is going back some years. Four? Five?"

Herman said, "Five."

"She said she was researching him for a book or some such garbage. We gave her what we had, which was practically nothing. She was cute. I kept her email, and we exchanged a couple of messages. But it never came to anything."

"Can you remember her name?"

He gazed at the blank wall. Hal said, "It was Olsen."

Jay said, "Yeah, Olsen, that's right. April Olsen was her name. Very cute."

NINE

We strolled down to the Flat Top, on the corner of West 121st, and sat outside at a small, wooden table under a parasol, staring at the traffic, eating cakes and drinking coffee in silence.

As usual it was Dehan who spoke first.

"So we can take it as read now that April was obsessed with Bernstein."

I turned my cup around a few times in the saucer.

"We can take it as read that she had a very active interest in him. I think we need more before we go as far as saying she was obsessed."

There was a hint of the sardonic in her tone of voice when she replied, "An interest that was active enough to make her buy his house and try to trace him to Central America."

I nodded, ignoring her tone. "Active enough for that."

"And we can take it that it was her interest in him that led to her death."

I stared awhile at the intricate, elegant, wrought iron balconies across the way, with their decorative shadows stretched across the wall beside the fire escape.

"Yeah," I said after a while, "but what we can't take as read is how . . ." I paused to think carefully about my words and concluded, " . . . how *causal* that link is. I mean, was her death a direct result of her curiosity? For example: she knew too much, she found out something, she found *him*, and therefore had to die . . ."

She was nodding. "Or was it more indirect. Her interest in him brought her into contact with people, or a situation, which led to her becoming a target."

"Precisely."

"Like . . ." She stared awhile at the tall, straggly trees across the road, beside the decorative wrought iron shadows. "It brought her into contact with Mexican drug dealers . . ." But she shook her head. "Nah," she concluded, "like nothing, we need more information."

"For a start we need to know who the guy in the shallow grave is. If we can eliminate Allan as one of the victims . . ."

My cell interrupted me, and I put it to my ear.

"Stone."

"Detective John Stone?"

"That's me. Who am I speaking to?"

"My name is Stella Bernstein. I have a message from my mother's retirement home that you wanted to speak to me and my sister about my father."

For a second I was stumped, then said, "Ah, yes, for some reason I was expecting you to be Braun . . ."

"My mother remarried. That was my stepfather's name. I retain my real father's name."

"Of course." I put it on speaker and placed it on the table between us. "Ms. Bernstein, I should explain the situation to you. I hope you don't find it too upsetting."

"I never knew my father, Detective, though I think I would have liked him. What has happened?"

"Do you recall that your mother sold a house that she had inherited from your father?"

She gave a small, pretty laugh. "Yes, we had a great holiday that year."

"Right, well, I am afraid a partially mummified body has been recovered from beneath the concrete in the basement of that house."

"Oh, my goodness!" Her shock sounded genuine. "But *mummified*? How?"

"It can happen naturally, if the conditions are right. The thing is, we are pretty sure it is not Professor Bernstein because he seems to have been in Mexico at the approximate time of death. But we need to be certain. And the only way we can be that, short of finding Professor Bernstein himself, is by comparing your DNA with that of the recovered body. Would you be willing to do that?"

"Of course I would. Would you need another from my sister? We are not on speaking terms, I'm afraid, but I can tell you how to contact her."

I shook my head, like she could see me. "No, that shouldn't be necessary. If you can give us an address, we can send a couple of officers over to collect a sample."

"Sure, I'll WhatsApp you my address. I'll be home all afternoon."

"Before you go, Ms. Bernstein, when we spoke to your mother, she was quite lucid."

"Yes, she has moments."

"She said something about a letter she had received from your father when he was in Mexico."

"Goodness, yes. She often mentioned it. Do you need it?"

"It would be extremely helpful, particularly if you still have the envelope."

"I can't promise, Detective, but I'll have a look."

I thanked her, and Dehan called Dispatch while I called Joe at the lab to tell him the sample would arrive that afternoon.

"How soon can you have it for me, Joe?"

"We already have his sample, so it's a straight one-to-one comparison. It won't take long."

"Thanks, I appreciate it."

I knew if Joe said it wouldn't take long, he meant to make sure it was fast. In the bad old days DNA testing could take weeks, but with the advances made by the University of Arizona and the UK's Forensic Science Service in microfluidics, waiting times were way down. I hung up.

"That's what I think Carl Jung would have called synchronicity."

"It's going to come back negative, you know that."

I nodded. "There's a pretty good chance, I grant you that."

"And when that happens . . ."

"If that happens."

"*If* that happens, then Allan Bernstein becomes our prime suspect."

I thought about it a moment as I swirled the remains around in circles at the bottom of my cup.

"I think he is already that, Dehan." I drained the coffee and set it down in the saucer. "If not him, then who?"

———

WE GOT BACK to the station house in time for a quick chat with Inspector John Newman, the chief. As we entered, in response to his, "Come!" he was, as always, watering his diminutive bonsai tree with a diminutive green tin watering can. And, as usual, he greeted us as though we were long-awaited, honored guests at a cocktail party.

"John," he said with pleasure, and carefully set down his watering can on a saucer. "Carmen, I've been meaning to chat with you and see how things are. Are you well? Are you happy?"

Dehan frowned, and I smiled. "Yes, sir, we are fine. We wanted to put you up to speed on the current case. It might get complicated."

"Indeed, sit, please. Make yourselves comfortable. Tell me what you need. Sit, sit." He sat himself with care in his leather chair. "This is the murder at Virgil Place, with the mummified corpse..."

"Yes, sir." It was Dehan, as she sat in a chair opposite the chief. "We are still waiting on forensics, but we feel there is a pretty good chance the body belongs to somebody murdered by Allan Bernstein, a professor at Columbia back in the eighties. He notoriously disappeared in Mexico at around the time our victim was killed."

He frowned at her and then at me. "Indeed, wasn't there also a young woman? How does she tie in?"

I drew breath, but Dehan beat me to it. "She was April Olsen, a lawyer in DC. Our working theory is that she found out he was still alive—his ex-wife had had him declared dead—and also the fact that he had killed whoever the victim was in the shallow grave. He killed her to silence her."

We went over the case again with him, fleshing out the details of Dehan's theory. He listened with care and made faces that suggested he thought we were on the right track. When we'd finished he said, "So what you want from me is to contact the Mexican *Guardia Nacional* and persuade them to put out a BOLO on Allan Bernstein."

I said, "And to check their records, particularly in Sonora. He seems to have had a special interest in visiting Sonora. There's a good chance he was arrested out there, at least once. By the sounds of it he was pretty wild and out of control when he left here."

"Good, well, I'll talk to them and see if we can persuade them to cooperate with us. Meantime, you have Simon Olsen to interview. He must be due to arrive. What do you hope to get from him?"

"I want to know what made her buy that house. It's not enough that she was obsessed. I think she was looking for something, and that's why she dug that hole in the cellar."

"You think she dug the hole, not her killer?"

I shook my head. "The ingrained dirt and cement indicates strongly that she was doing the digging. And she dug it up at least several hours before she was killed. Possibly days before. Because she was showered and clean, and she had dressed for some kind of date."

The inspector's desk phone buzzed. He picked up the receiver and smiled as he listened. When he was done he said, "Thank you, Maria. I'll tell them." He hung up. "Simon Olsen, he is in interview room number three."

We left the inspector reaching for the phone to call a contact in Mexico and crossed the floor to the interrogation rooms by way of the coffee machine. Dehan pushed in ahead of me holding three paper cups in two hands and deposited them on the old Formica and steel tubing table, while Simon Olsen watched her, then glanced nervously at me. I smiled pleasantly back.

As I sat I said, "Before anything else, Mr. Olsen, I want to thank you for coming in. I know this is a very hard time for you and, though it is a formula, I am genuinely very sorry for your loss."

That seemed to throw him for a moment and he said, "Um . . ." several times. I thought I'd move it along and asked, "Have you been able to identify . . . ?"

He nodded. "Yes. It is her. There is no doubt. Poor Mommy almost passed out. I have left her at the hotel, to rest."

"Mr. Olsen, we have very reliable evidence indicating that your sister had developed some kind of fascination . . ." I glanced at Dehan. "I don't think that is too strong a word. A fascination with Professor Allan Bernstein."

"Him again?"

Dehan smiled. "I'm afraid so. It seems this case revolves around Professor Bernstein. Your sister's body was found in the house he had owned, and which she bought from his ex-wife. And we have learned today that she was actively investigating his disappearance, and trying to trace him."

There was a short pause. He didn't look like he was about to say anything so I asked him, "Mr. Olsen, I find it hard to believe that she never spoke to you about any of this."

"Well, I suppose she did, but I never took it seriously. I thought it was just her being stupid. She was very stupid sometimes."

"She told you about her interest in Professor Bernstein? How long ago was this?"

He made a face and hunched his shoulders.

"I don't know."

I sighed and felt suddenly tired. "Well, Mr. Olsen, we can state definitely that it wasn't the day she was born and it wasn't yesterday. So start narrowing from there and give me a not more than, not less than."

He blinked a few times like he was having trouble adjusting to the idea.

"Well, I suppose we were in our teens."

Dehan's eyebrows shot up. "She became interested in Professor Bernstein in her teens?"

"Yes. We heard a few stories about him. I thought he sounded like a rather stupid man who arrived twenty years too late to the party." He smiled from me to Dehan like he'd said something clever. "I mean," he added, "you don't actually need a PhD to take drugs and spout off a lot of nonsense about expanded consciousness and free love, do you? I had his number from the start."

"But April?"

"April said she thought he was cool, and started asking Mommy and Daddy about him all the time, until it started to get on Mommy's nerves and she told her to drop it."

I asked, "And did she?"

"Not really, except that I suppose she stopped talking to Mom and Dad about it so much. She still talked to me. Mommy had told her that he had gone to Mexico, and she wanted to know where. Mom told her she had no idea. She had friends who had known him, but she didn't know him herself. So April begged her and nagged her for the names of those friends."

Dehan asked, "Did she give them to her?"

"I don't know. You have to remember, back then I thought this was all just a very stupid phase she was going through."

Dehan grabbed her long hair and tied it in a knot behind her neck. While she did this she asked, "Where'd your sister go to college?"

"Harvard. She did law at Harvard."

I smiled. "Not that stupid, then."

He shrugged. "I guess, but she could be real stupid sometimes. When she got an idea fixed in her mind, there was no way of shaking her."

"What about you?"

"I went to Columbia, like Mom and Dad."

"And did you have much contact during that time?"

He picked up his coffee and peered into it, like he was scared it was going to bite him.

"Hardly. Thanksgiving, Christmas, that was about it. We didn't have the same kind of friends, and we certainly didn't move in the same circles."

Dehan said, "So she graduated and . . ."

"Oh, she was headhunted from Harvard by Groves and Feinstein, into their international trade department. She was very scornful of the work Mom and Dad did, very patronizing and quite spiteful sometimes. She said they were hypocrites and fakes."

"So during this time, what happened with her interest in Professor Bernstein?"

"I don't know. As I say, I had practically no contact with her."

I scratched my head. "But she *did* tell you she had bought the house."

"Yes. She called me from New York and told me she wanted to show me something. It was very unusual. She was very rarely friendly to me, but she said she wanted to have lunch and show me what she'd bought. She gave me an address to drive to, in the

Bronx! Imagine my consternation! And when I got there and she came out and took me inside . . . my goodness!"

"What did she say to you?"

"She asked me if I knew what it was. I said, 'Well, it's a house!' And a rather nasty, vulgar one! And she said yes, but did I know which house? I'm afraid I haven't much patience with nonsense and I told her so, and she told me then that it was Allan Bernstein's house!"

I drummed my fingers on the table for a moment, then asked, "And I imagine you asked her what had made her buy it."

"Damn right!" He stared at me as though I had said something shocking and repeated, "Damn right I did! Only I didn't phrase it quite as politely as that. 'What the *hell* do you think you're doing?' would be closer to the mark. 'Are you out of your *tiny* skull?'"

Dehan cut in. "Yeah, I bet you got real tough on her. What did she say?"

He sighed and looked around at the walls.

"I mean, it didn't make a lot of sense. As far as I am concerned, she was out of her mind. She started going crazy as a teen, and just got crazier as she got older . . ."

"What did she say, Mr. Olsen?"

He hesitated and faltered, blinking and shaking his head. "That she wanted to be close to him. That he was one of the great thinkers of the twentieth century, that he stood for values that had been lost, ideals that had been squandered, she said, and I don't know what more nonsense. And she wanted to have the house that he had inhabited, so that she could be close to him."

I scratched my head, thinking about what he'd said and how he'd phrased it.

"So, did she go to Mexico to look for him?"

"I can't tell you for certain, but I think she did, and not just once. I think she went a couple of times."

"But she didn't tell you about it."

"No, not directly, no."

Dehan shook her head. "What does that mean, not directly?"

His cheeks colored and he gave a silly laugh that was almost a giggle.

"I mean, she may have hinted and insinuated that she might go and look for him, or that she had already..."

"Something I don't understand, Mr. Olsen," I said, "and forgive me for interrupting, is, does it strike you as odd that she would actually arrange for you to go and see the house she had bought to be closer to her idol, and yet keep it a secret that she had been to Mexico, looking for him?"

I thought the question would faze him, but it didn't. His eyebrows arched in a "there you go!" sort of way and he spread his hands.

"That is *exactly* what I am talking about. This is April all over. And do you know why she did it? Shall I tell you why she behaved like that? Because she was a narcissist. Because she *needed*—it was a physical *need*—for all the attention to be on her. If everyone wasn't looking at her, listening to her crackpot ideas, and above all *talking* about her, she could not stand it! It drove her crazy. So she would create situations that guaranteed that *she* and nobody else was the absolute center of attention."

I thought about it, staring at the wall, while Dehan pressed him.

"I want you to think very carefully about this before you answer, Mr. Olsen. When April made these hints and these comments about Mexico, when would that have been?"

"Oh, well, I mean, it went on for quite a while, but I suppose it might have been about five years ago. You know, it might have been six, I could not be absolutely certain."

I kept watching him, mulling over what he was saying, trying to visualize it happening. Dehan was asking him, "Did she ever mention any people, or any places in particular..."

He became abstracted and leaned back in his chair.

"This has been very stressful, I think I will have to go soon."

"If you could just answer that one question before you go..."

"Yes." He nodded but looked ill. "Yes, she mentioned some people. Two friends of Bernstein's who could help her." Dehan glanced at me. He went on. "One of them had an Irish name, O'Mahoney, and like the computer in that film, Hal, Hal O'Mahoney. And the other one was Russian sounding. He was the one she thought might be most helpful. Petrovich, something like that. She said she was corresponding with them and that the Russian one was being very helpful. He had told her a place in Mexico where Bernstein might have gone."

Dehan said, "And she went there."

"I think so."

"Can you remember the place?"

"Oh, it was one of those corny names you hear in the movies, like Santa Cruz, El Paso, Sonora . . ." He took a swig of his coffee and made a face. "Oh my Lord, that is awful! Sonora. It was a town in Sonora. I can't tell you any more, and I really must go or I fear I might get ill. I have high blood pressure, you know."

He hesitated, looking from one to the other of us.

"Is that okay, can I go now?"

I spread my hands. "Of course, thank you for all your help, Mr. Olsen."

He stood and made his way rather jerkily to the door, then stopped and looked back at us.

"Tuliacan? No, Tuli, something with Tuli. Turicachi, about fifty miles south of Douglas." His lips worked silently for a moment. "El . . . El Brujo? That was the guy he was going to meet down there. El Brujo. I do want to help . . ."

He opened the door and left, on slightly unsteady feet.

TEN

"El Brujo just means the warlock, the magician. Probably some kind of shaman who services that village, Turicachi. He was trying to live out the Carlos Castaneda fantasy in some way. After all, he was, what, forty-something in the eighties? That makes him twenty-something in the sixties. He was at college when that whole scene was going down, man."

Dehan was sitting with her boots crossed on the corner of her desk and her arms crossed over her chest. I was standing with my hands in my pants pockets, watching her. She chewed her lip for a bit, then added, "Douglas, that's Arizona, thirty, forty miles from the state line with New Mexico."

"As the crow flies."

"Yeah, not a lot of roads down there. Most folks travel either by horse or UFO."

I leaned over my chair and brought up Google Earth.

"The only road of any size down there is the Arizona 80. If he came from New Mexico, it means he crossed the state line at Rodeo."

She nodded silently for a bit. "Doesn't mean he was living there, though. What county is that?"

I read from the screen. "Unincorporated, census designated . .

. Hidalgo County. The sheriff is all the way up in Lordsburg. About forty-five miles away."

"I'll give them a call."

While she dialed, I stared at the satellite images, trying to visualize him down there. As I did so I spoke absently.

"Why do you think Mahoney and Petrov misled us?"

She listened to the ringtone for a moment and answered me, also absently.

"Because we are establishment pigs and they are rebels with one foot in the sixties and the other in the grave."

I made a "hmmm" sound. She went on.

"Also, they're college smart, and they figure that if we're homicide cops and we're looking for Bernstein, there's a good chance we want to pin a homicide on him. They don't know where he is —*probably* don't know where he is—but he's their pal, their hero, the guy who did what they could only dream of doing, so they don't want to feed him to the pigs."

"Yeah, I guess. Petrov was sweet on April."

She frowned at me. "Is that relevant?" Before I could answer she sat forward and said, "Oh, hi, good afternoon, this is Detective Carmen Dehan of the New York Police Department . . ."

I zoned out and sat down in my chair, looking at the scorched red-and-ochre earth of Arizona and New Mexico, wondering where he had stayed and where he had gone. And if he was still there. And above all, what had made April go after him.

No answers came, so after a while I closed down the program and started searching for men between thirty and fifty, disappeared in New York between 1984 and 1986. There were surprisingly few unaccounted for, and none of those fit the description of the guy in the shallow grave. I had widened my search a couple of times, without success, when Dehan hung up.

"They couldn't tell me anything except Rodeo is a small, quiet town. They barely have any kind of problems, and what they do have they sort out themselves. Sheriff goes down from time to time to say hi, but he isn't aware of any newcomers to the area."

I sat back in my chair and waved a hand at the screen. "I can't find any promising matches..."

"You through with me already?"

I smiled. "I'm looking for men who went missing around eighty-four to eighty-six and were never found. There are surprisingly few, and I haven't found anyone so far who could be our guy. If we don't get a match from Stella..." I trailed off, not quite sure what we were going to do if we didn't get a match from Stella. Dehan had no such uncertainty.

"If we don't get a match with Stella we take a powder to New Mexico, *compadre*, and then to Turicachi, Mexico."

I planted a one-sided smile on one side of my face. "Girl loves a road trip, but to be honest, I don't see the inspector authorizing this one, Dehan."

She shrugged, made a face, and shook her head, all in rapid sequence.

"If he doesn't, Stone, we're screwed. We have a lot of who what and maybe, but I don't see that we have a single lead that actually leads anywhere, apart from Allan Bernstein in Mexico. We need him."

I sighed. "We still have unexplored avenues, but I just can't get a handle on this one, Dehan. I mean, if his wife inherited everything, what the hell is he living on in Mexico? I can't see the..." I hesitated, searching for the word, then blurted out, "The gestalt!"

"The who now?"

"Bring a series of objects or circumstances together and they will often form more than the sum of their parts."

"Uh-huh..."

"Beethoven's Ninth, it's really just a lot of noises, but they come together in such a way that they become more than the sum of their parts."

"I get it."

"Usually, a homicide is like that, all the bits and pieces fit together in some way and I get a *feel* for the gestalt. But this one, it's just a bunch of random, slightly bizarre facts that don't really link up. Or appear not to." Dehan drew breath to answer, but I plowed on. "I mean, either whoever killed April camped out in her place while he dug up the body, and then killed her, or, as the forensics suggest, April, after spending years popping in and out of the house, suddenly decided to dig up the cellar, go out to dinner, and bring her date back to see her mummy . . ."

"Whole new spin on come and meet the folks."

"Quite, and her date was so upset that he shot her."

"With the same gun the mummy was shot with."

"Exactly. Even if we say that her date was Bernstein, it does not explain why she decided to dig up the cellar after all those years. There is something fundamental missing here, a crucial piece that we are overlooking."

Dehan narrowed her eyes the way she did when she was thinking hard.

"Maybe," she said, and my phone rang.

"Yeah, Stone."

"Detective Stone, this is Stella Bernstein."

"Oh, hi, how can I help you?"

"I just thought I'd tell you that the police officers have been and taken the swab, and also that I found the letter my father sent my mother from Mexico. I am looking after most of her stuff, and they were with her old correspondence. It was the last communication she ever had with him. There was another letter with it, sent from New Mexico. I have scanned them both; if you give me your email address I'll send them over."

"That would be excellent, Ms. Bernstein. With scans of the envelopes too, front and back, if that's okay."

"Of course. Glad to be of help. And please, call me Stella."

"That's very kind, thank you, Stella."

I hung up, and Dehan arched an eyebrow at me.

"Stella? Do we have a picture of this Stella?"

"Only in my head."

"I could come over and do grievous physical damage to you, Stone."

"What? In my image she is eight feet tall and has no teeth, and big hairy warts on her nose." She screwed up a small piece of paper and threw it at me. "Violence!" I protested. "Always the violence, she employs! What happened to dialogue, and compromise?"

"Shut up, Stone. I was saying, before your new girlfriend phoned, that maybe we should take a closer look at Itchy and Scratchy over at Columbia." She held up a hand. "Before you interrupt, think about it. You yourself noted that they lied about their contact with April Olsen. Their relationship with Bernstein was close and, for all we know, intimate . . ."

"That's true, Dehan, but aside from Jay Petrov misrepresenting his contact with April . . ."

"They both did, Stone. Let me remind you what Simon Olsen said when I asked if she ever mentioned any particular places or people."

"Remind me."

"He said there were two friends of Bernstein's who could help her, one of them had an Irish name, O'Mahoney like the computer in *2001: A Space Odyssey*. That was obviously Hal Mahoney. The other one was Russian sounding, and he was the one she thought might be most helpful. He said it was something like Petrovich, obviously Petrov. He said she told him she was corresponding with *them* and that the Russian one was being very helpful. That ties in with what Petrov himself told us. Also, he specifically said that Petrov had told her a place in Mexico where Bernstein might have gone. Don't forget, Stone, that we got the name from Olsen, but he got it from Itchy and Scratchy, albeit via April."

"That's true, Dehan."

"So maybe they're not just fobbing us off because we are establishment fascist pigs. Maybe they're fobbing us off because they are actively trying to conceal their part in some kind of crazy Charles Manson murder. Who knows, maybe when she tracked Bernstein down and spoke to him, he told her all about it. Maybe he needed to confess, or he was boasting! Who knows? Point is, she came back, dug up the evidence, confronted Petrov and Mahoney, the dynamic duo, and one or both of them killed her." She paused, then added, "We need their alibis for the night of the murder."

My computer told me I had mail. It was from Stella Bernstein. I opened the attachments and printed two copies of each. While I was collecting the printouts Dehan said, "It must be Christmas. We just got her financials and her phone records too." She reached out a hand. "Let's have a look while they print."

I handed her a print of each envelope and each of the letters, then sat to examine them while the printer hummed in the background. Dehan smiled.

"Letters. I guess in the eighties people still wrote each other letters. You should write me sometimes."

I frowned at her. "We're married. We live together. In the same house."

She grinned. "And you know what? You should use a fountain pen. And start, 'My Dearest Carmen, as I sit here at my desk, gazing upon the moors, my thoughts turn ever to thee . . .' That would be cool."

"If I do that, will you wear a drawstring blouse and carry a milk churn on your hip?"

She waggled her eyebrows and picked up the letters. "Focus!" she said.

The envelopes were very similar, addressed in firm uppercase, except that one bore a U.S. stamp and was postmarked September 28, 1985, Rodeo, New Mexico, and the other was postmarked October 15, 1985, Esqueda, Sonora.

I took the first letter. It was brief, in a large, self-indulgent scrawl with lots of loops.

Hey Babe, I know you don't give a damn, all you care about is your bourgeois aspirations, but fact is, for some reason, you are the only woman who ever inspired or challenged me. I know that inside you is the spirit of an eagle, babe. So when my mind is on fire, I think of you. That should please you, and you should fly to me.

I'm in New Mex, it's wild, wild country here and I like it. You can really trip at night, and you would not believe how high you can go up among those cold, cold stars and look down on the desert. It's crazy. I can see you here. I can see us here. I want you to come and join me.

But you know what? I have spent my whole goddamn life teaching others, and now I need somebody to teach me.

Some pals here, who sell me the peyote, they told me there is a "brujo" down in Sonora who's the real deal, and I'm going to go down and see if I can find him. You should come too, babe, and we can write that damned book together. And be free.

You have to come.

Allan

THEN I TOOK the second letter, which was written in the same, large hand.

Hey, listen, I know what you think about Columbia. And maybe you're right. But believe me, when I am done with this research, when I write my book, they will be getting down on their knees, begging me to come back. Not just Columbia, Harvard, Oxford, the fucking CIA! When I discover the portal to altered states of consciousness, when I discover the doorway that allows the human mind to fly and flow freely wherever it will go, unencumbered by the flesh, then I will be hailed as the man who freed humanity. Fear not for me, for I am on the path of freedom!

I know the place where I have to go, I know the place where I have to be, and I know who must be there with me. I have learned the shaman's name. They call him "El Brujo," the warlock, and I'll

be meeting with him in just a few days. That will be a time of destiny. Then all will be transformed...
    Allan

I heard Dehan mutter, "Boy, this guy was really away with the fairies..."

I ignored the comment and said, "Twenty-eighth of September, and then the fifteenth of October. That's seventeen days, almost three weeks."

She glanced up at me. "So?" She shrugged. "What struck me more was the way in the first letter he is all about her. He wants to fix things, and he wants her to go down there with him."

I nodded. "There is a definite change in tone. It may not mean much. Guys get like that when they are drunk. I guess it's the same when they're high. They think back on all their exes and each one of them was the only one they ever really loved."

"Really?" She didn't sound amused.

"I'm afraid so. Marie was obviously familiar with it and poured cold water on it, because he's given up in the second letter."

"I guess."

"But this..." I tapped the two dates with my finger. "Doesn't that seem a long time to you? It's not like he needs to clear his schedule. And in the first letter, he seems keen, eager. 'He's the real deal,' 'I'm going to go down, see if I can find him,' here, 'in a few days.' He sounds keen."

She shrugged. "So it took him two and a half weeks to write. It doesn't mean it took him two and a half weeks to get there. He might have been there a couple of weeks already when he wrote that."

I stared at it a moment. It was true there was nothing in the letter that said he was still in New Mexico, and yet...

"But, in this letter, the second one"—I held it up—"he still hasn't met this brujo guy. You know it's only about a hundred miles from Rodeo to Turicachi. Taking it easy it's just a couple of hours' drive."

"So what?"

"I don't know. If he was so motivated, why did he hang around so much? It doesn't seem to fit."

"Like everything else in this goddamn case. We need to persuade the chief, go down, talk to the people there, and *find* this guy. It's the only way we are going to get any movement at all."

The printer stopped disgorging April's financials, and Dehan went over to collect them. A moment later she dumped a fistful of pages on the desk and dropped back into her chair. I kept staring at the two letters in front of me. I read through the second one four or five times, comparing it with the first. The tone was different, and the insistence that she should join him was gone, but the content was all but identical in each. He also briefly addressed the issue of getting canned by the university in the second. But there was nothing new as far as the actual content was concerned. Yet almost three weeks had passed.

The date. I stared at the two dates. Twenty-eighth to the fifteenth. Seventeen days.

I picked up the letters and the envelopes and showed them to Dehan. "This," I said.

"What?" She looked up from the financials and frowned.

"*This* is the gestalt. We answer this, we break the case. Everything is here."

"What are you talking about, Stone? There isn't even a question. Answer what?"

"Oh, there *is*, my dearest Carmen, there is."

"*What?*"

"Precisely! What made him delay seventeen days in making a two-hour trip that he was desperate to make? *That* is the question!"

ELEVEN

We spent the rest of the afternoon trawling through five years' worth of financial records and established that April had traveled to both New Mexico and old Mexico several times in the last half decade. We made a note of the dates, and the only significant pattern we could find was that her trips tended to coincide with holiday periods. The other significant thing about them was that her trips tended to be a flight to Phoenix, and then a hire car with stops at gas stations south of the city on the I-10. South from Phoenix on the I-10 takes you past Tucson and eventually to Benson. Hang a right there onto the AZ 80 and that takes you right down to Douglas, Esqueda, and Turicachi. It fit.

I also noted, in my mental notebook, that the night she was killed she had indeed been out to dinner, at the Ulivo in Greenwich Village, and had paid with her Amex card.

It was late by the time we stepped out of the station house and made our way to the old Jag. I threw Dehan the keys, bent over backward, and crunched my vertebrae. "You drive," I said, "you're younger than I am."

She caught the keys with a left-handed swipe and said, "I was. I think I'm catching up." As she opened the door and climbed behind the wheel she added, "You know? If I was ten and you were twenty, I'd be half your age."

I climbed in beside her and slammed the door. "I knew that."

She fired up the old growler and carried on. "But ten years later I'd be twenty and you'd be thirty. So I'd be two-thirds your age."

I frowned. "Hmmm..."

She reversed out of the lot. "Ten years after that I'm thirty and you're forty, so I am three-quarters your age, and ten years after *that* I am forty and you are fifty so I am *four-fifths* your age! So eventually, given enough time, not only will I be the same age as you, I will be *older* than you. How does that work?"

"Dehan, I think you need a drink."

My cell rang, and it was Joe.

"John, I stayed late doing your comparison with the mummy and Bernstein's daughter."

I put it on speaker, said to Dehan, "It's Joe. He's run the comparison with Stella." To the phone I said, "What did you get, Joe?"

"They are not related in any way. I have no idea who the guy in the grave is, John, but I can tell you categorically that it is not Professor Allan Bernstein."

"Okay, Joe. Thanks for putting in the extra hours. I appreciate it. I owe you."

He laughed. "Yeah, you owe me so much it would be cruel to collect. Take it easy, pal."

We drove in silence for a while, watching the dead and dying shop fronts slide by in a lugubrious procession of listless, yellow lights spilled onto solitary pedestrians like forgotten hopes across barren sidewalks and blacktop.

"We go to Mexico," she said, eventually. I glanced at her, saw light wash up her body and across her face. I nodded. She went on. "But first we talk to Petrov again and ask him why he lied about April. He knew Bernstein was in Mexico. He knew *where* in Mexico and he told April. Hell! Two gets you twenty he knew *why*

Bernstein was in Mexico, and he can name the mummy in that grave."

"Agreed." I gently thumped my knee with my palm a couple of times. "So first order of business tomorrow is a talk with the chief. If he refuses permission to go to Mexico, we're going to have to work on Petrov till he cracks. I don't think that will be easy."

"I agree, but there's a chance—an outside chance—that if we go for Mahoney as well, we can play them against each other."

I grunted agreement and sat turning my cell over in my fingers, looking at it from all angles. There was one thought that kept nagging at me.

"I want to see the house again," I said. "This case . . . it's all about the sixties. It's all about Don Juan, altered states of consciousness . . ." I shook my head, trying to find the precise definition. "It's all about Professor Allan Bernstein and his obsessive search. Would you agree?"

"Sure." She glanced at me. "Of course."

"So much so that the second victim, April, bought his house and obsessively kept it exactly as he had had it."

She smiled. "So now she *is* obsessive?"

I ignored her and went on. "And we've been going crazy asking ourselves, what made her do that? Why'd she buy it and leave it as it was all that time? And yet, here we are, aside from a cursory glance on the night of the murder, we haven't gone near the place. We need to go there and find what it was . . ."

I faltered, not sure how to finish, but Dehan finished for me.

"What it was that kept her there, that kept her coming back, that drove her in the end to dig in the cellar. We need to look for what she was looking for. I agree. You're right."

We turned onto Morris Park, and I watched again the play of light and shadow across her face. After a moment I said, "So, first thing in the morning the chief, then we go look at the house, see if we can find anything that lends a little more strength to your theory." She glanced at me, and I smiled. "It's your theory. You take the credit. Then we go lean on Petrov a bit, see how he reacts. After that, armed with whatever we can get out of him, we go to Mexico, New and old, provided the chief gives us the okay."

She wagged her head up and down a few times, then flashed me a smile. "That's the sequence, big guy. You are pooped. Martini, pizza, bed."

I closed my eyes with a smug grin on my face. "Especially bed," I said.

———

As so often happens, in the morning I saw things differently, and, at seven a.m., as I dipped my bacon into my egg yolk and shoved it in my mouth, watching Dehan refill her cup with black coffee, I said, "Screw it, let's go wake Petrov up and give him a scare. Where does he live? Let's go to his house and wake the arrogant little toad up and give him a shake. See if he ribbits."

She made a gurgling chuckle sound in her throat, almost like a ribbit.

"I see the sleep did you good. I've got his address in the file. As I recall he's got one of those nice brownstones in Brooklyn Heights, on Henry Street."

"Good, let's go rattle his cage."

"Ain't you mixin' your metaphors there, Sensei?"

"The hell with my metaphors!" I growled. "I'm feelin' crazy today!" I held out my cup. "Fill me up, Carmen."

Jay Petrov had a big old brownstone at the south end of Henry Street, half a block from State Street. It was on the seedy side of elegant, with chipped stucco and an unruly vine climbing over the door at the top of the stoop. But from what I could see through the window, as Dehan rang the big brass bell, the inside was more on the elegant side of seedy. The glass was made dark by the early-morning sun, but I could make out French doors open onto a luminous green lawn, and sofas and big armchairs that were carelessly eclectic in a way only really expensive things can be.

The door was opened by a dark-haired girl in her early twenties wearing Levi's and a Columbia University sweatshirt. She had pretty eyes and a mouth that knew it was kissable. She studied me a second, then turned to Dehan.

"Good morning, can I help you?"

There was an accent, but I wasn't going to try and nail it. We showed her our badges and I said, "Is Professor Petrov at home?"

She tried to hide the smile, but it was obvious she'd done this before and it still amused her.

"Which one, please? Professor Margaret Petrov, or Professor Jay Petrov?"

I couldn't think of a wiseass thing to say, but Dehan said, "I figure they both have long hair, so let's have the one who's bald on top."

The girl looked startled, so I said, "Professor Jay Petrov."

"He is having the breakfast now."

Dehan smiled. "Good, mine's black, no sugar. Detective Stone's is the same. Show us to the breakfast room." She stepped over the threshold, and as the girl started to protest she said, "By the way, what's your name?"

"Maria, but . . ."

Dehan talked as she walked. "Maria, that's a nice name. My name is Maria too. Maria del Carmen. Where are you from, Maria?"

"Poland, but . . ."

"Poland, huh? I hear you have nice cabbages in Poland. This way? Through here? Thanks. Remember, black, no sugar. The big guy is the same. Good morning, Professors Petrov."

We had crossed a large, tiled entrance hall crammed with very old, very expensive furniture that was trying very hard not to be ostentatious. We had gone past a magnificent set of walnut doors that offered a glimpse of a large, spacious drawing room, down a passage, and into a sunny conservatory with millions of flowers of all conceivable colors and a breakfast table set with white linen, silver, and china, and seated on two wicker armchairs were the two Professor Petrovs, both looking startled.

Jay Petrov was once again in a cream linen suit with a blue shirt and his long hair tied into a ponytail. He was half-turned in his seat with a piece of toast halfway to his mouth, and he was scowling.

Margaret Petrov was attractive in her early fifties. She had abundant red hair, which did whatever it liked on her head, and bright blue eyes that were not unamused, but wanted to know who we were and why we were there. We obliged by holding up our badges. I said, "Your very good health. Forgive us for barging in on your breakfast. It's a matter of some urgency, as we'll be leaving for Mexico later today, and we wanted to speak with you, Professor Petrov, before we went."

Professor Margaret Petrov's eyes swiveled from mine to her husband's. Her left eyebrow made an arch that probably congealed his blood, and she dabbed at her lips with her napkin.

"Jay...?"

He looked back at me and blustered. "You can't just..."

"If it's more convenient for you, we can talk at the station. We could send a car to pick you up, if you like."

He made to stand. "This is harassment..."

I cut him short. "Not at all. We are very grateful to you for your help, and aim to cause you as little embarrassment as possible."

Professor Margaret Petrov leaned back in her chair and offered me the same arched eyebrow she had offered her husband moments before. It didn't congeal my blood. It made me smile. She said, "Perhaps you'd better sit down, Detectives. I didn't catch your names. Coffee?"

"That's very kind of you. Detectives John Stone and Carmen Dehan. We won't keep you long." I smiled down at Jay and noticed that the top of his head had turned red. "We have a few more questions about Professor Bernstein and the young lady who was searching for him. You remember you mentioned her?"

"This is intolerable!"

Dehan narrowed her eyes at him.

"It's a murder inquiry. A double homicide. Is there some reason you don't want to cooperate with us, Professor?"

"No! Of course there isn't! I just object to you . . ."

"Shall we get it over and done with then? We are also busy."

Margaret dropped her napkin on the table beside her plate.

"I have to go to work. I shall leave you to it." She smiled a smile of ice at her husband. "You can tell me all about it when I get home, dear. It had better be good."

She stood, and I watched her walk from the conservatory with an attractive swing of her hips. She left a resounding silence behind her. I sat beside Jay Petrov and smiled at him.

"Not a sixties child, huh?"

Dehan pulled up a chair opposite mine and leaned her elbows on the white linen.

"Why'd you lie to us, Jay?"

"I don't have to put up with this!"

Dehan's face creased into a thin smile with narrowed eyes. "See? You kind of do. Because you lied about your relationship with a girl who later turned up as the victim in a homicide, in your best pal's house. But here's the thing, right now you're not a prime suspect. We just want an explanation. Lawyer up, keep lying, keep dodging, and you will make it to the number one spot real fast. So you need to ask yourself, how bad do you want to see patrol cars showing up on Amsterdam Avenue with their lights and their sirens going? Or better still, here, on quiet, leafy Henry Street."

"This is blackmail!"

I shook my head. "It's fair warning, Professor Petrov. There is nothing illegal in what we are doing or saying. It is, however, illegal to lie to the police and conceal evidence, and it is particularly serious in a homicide investigation. Now, I am going to ask you one more time, what made you lie to us about that girl?"

"I didn't lie."

Dehan sat back in her chair. She was still smiling. "You're going to have to explain that, Jay."

His sigh was more like a groan. He leaned forward and covered his face with his hands. After a moment he emerged from his safe, dark place, but his face was as red as the top of his head.

"There is really nothing to explain," he explained. "She . . ."

I cut across him. "Remind me, what was her name?"

He looked at me along his eyes and sighed again.

"April. I used to joke with her that one day I'd take her to Paris and finally have . . ."

He faltered, and Dehan supplied the rest.

"April in Paris?"

"Yeah, it sounds lame now. It was fun at the time."

I said, "So, you were going to explain."

"She contacted me, oh, it must be five years ago, maybe a little more. She was fascinated by Allan. The man's charisma and magnetism is extraordinary. Even after all this time, he just seems to bewitch people."

He paused, licked his lips, and made a gesture of helplessness. "Anyway, I guess I exploited her fascination and placed myself in his limelight. I'm a sucker for a pretty woman. I can't help myself. So we exchanged a few emails, mainly about Allan, and eventually I invited her to come to see me at my office at the university. She was as pretty as her picture. And smart with it. Not book smart, though she was that too. She was truly *intelligent*. Her mind was alive, curious, penetrating. There was something reckless about her too, which was very attractive."

"So what happened?" It was Dehan.

He looked momentarily disgusted.

"Sitting here, talking to you, it sounds tawdry, banal, but it wasn't. It was exciting and beautiful." He looked Dehan in the eye.

Then he turned and looked at me. "You see, I loved Allan. It wasn't a homosexual thing. I really loved him. He was unique, a one-off. They made him and they threw away the mold. And when April came along, searching for him, I guess I found a way to express the love I felt for him, by loving her. She was magical, passionate." He sat forward with his palm held out, like he was showing us something. "Her intellect—I work with some of the finest intellects in the U.S.A., or anywhere. I am surrounded, day in and day out, by intellectual giants. I myself have an IQ of one hundred and fifty. But all of us, I include myself, have achieved this intellectual prowess at the *expense* of our emotional freedom. We chain and bind our emotional selves so that our intellectual selves can fly, soar, up into the heavens of analysis." He shook his head. "But April, her intellect was *in the service* of her passion. She was first and foremost a passionate being." He sank back and spread his hands. "I guess that's why she was so fascinated by Allan. Because he was the same. Where we academics are slaves to our intellects, his intellect was his slave."

Dehan was frowning.

"So, you had an affair."

He snorted. "If you want to call it that. We were close, and we often had sex. Does that count as an affair?"

She nodded. "Yeah. It does. How long did it last?"

He made a face that suggested the question was a stupid one.

"It never ended. It was just there. All the time."

I cleared my throat. "Did your wife object?"

"She doesn't know about it. That is one of the great differences between me and Allan, and April. They have that courage. I haven't."

I pressed. "So, where did you meet?"

"If Margaret was away at a conference or something, she would come here. If I was away, she would often accompany me. Sometimes I visited her in Washington."

"You ever go to Mexico together?"

He closed his eyes. After a while he said, "Yes, a few times."

"What for?"

"To look for Allan."

"So you did know where he was."

He started to speak several times, but his voice failed him. Finally he said, irritably, "I told her I knew. Okay, I'm a shit! But I was scared of losing her. So I told her I knew where he was. I knew if she believed that she would stay with me." He stared down at his open palms. "It wasn't exactly a lie. I kind of knew. I knew he'd been in Sonora, in a small village called Turicachi. He'd found a brujo down there who was going to teach him all about peyote and ayahuasca. He was real excited."

I asked, "He told you that himself?"

"Yeah, we talked on the phone. I was going to go and visit him." He shrugged. "But he went off the radar. When April turned up, I thought it'd be a gas to go down and see if we could find him."

"But you didn't find him."

"No, we didn't find him."

TWELVE

The yellow-and-black crime scene tape rose slightly on the morning breeze, then sagged, like it couldn't be bothered to try anymore. We ducked under the tape and unlocked the door, stepped into the shady quiet, and closed it behind us with a clunk. I was suddenly acutely aware of being in a private, intimate place, a place that had belonged exclusively to two people who had touched each other across space and time, without ever having met.

Dehan spoke softly. "I wouldn't admit this to anyone but you, Stone, but this place gives me the creeps."

I nodded. "It's dark, kiddo. Whatever happened here, it was very dark. You want to take the living room? I'll start on the bedrooms."

"Sure."

She snapped on her latex gloves and made her way on her long, slim legs into the gloom of the living room. I pulled on my gloves and climbed the stairs.

Upstairs were the bathroom and the four bedrooms I had seen before. The bathroom still showed the same signs of minimal use as before, plus what the crime scene guys had done. The single, almost unused tube of toothpaste and the toothbrush were gone. They had showed us that nobody had been camping here, waiting to kill her. It was she who had been camping here, waiting to be killed.

The bathroom cabinet was also empty, its contents gone to the lab. I muttered to myself, "If only I knew what I was looking for . . ." I closed the cabinet door and saw myself looking back at me. "If only you knew what you were looking for," my reflection repeated at me.

I remembered Dehan scowling at the long blond hair in the brush. She had said, "That makes sense to you? Long blond hair makes sense to you? How?"

I had said something about a Hells Angel, and April herself. But Petrov had long blond hair too, even though he was bald on top. Was he a Hells Angel, with a small *a*?

I shook my head then shrugged and went to look at the bedrooms.

It was pretty much as I remembered it. The master bedroom and the two larger rooms had the mattresses wrapped in plastic. The drapes were drawn closed and there was a stench of tired, old damp. I went through the drawers again and found what I had found the first time: nothing. The wardrobes were still empty too. There were no shoeboxes with recently fired revolvers in them.

Downstairs I could hear Dehan moving about and for a moment wondered whether Allan Bernstein, or his pal Jay Petrov, had ever sat up here and listened to April moving around downstairs, putting on an old vinyl, pouring a drink or rolling a joint.

I moved to the fourth, smaller room. The bed had been stripped by the crime scene team. On the floor there were signs they had swept up samples of dirt and concrete from the floor beside the bed.

April had camped out here while she dug a hole downstairs? My mind struggled to visualize the set of bizarre circumstances that had led to that situation: a successful, talented lawyer specializing in international trade, living and working in DC, buys a house in the Bronx, hardly uses it, and after almost a decade she digs up the cellar and finds a mummified corpse. How did she find out it was there? Who told her? And whose body was it?

I opened the wardrobe and looked inside. Like everything else, it was empty. What was she looking for in this house?

I heard the tread of Dehan's boots on the stairs and watched her approach across the landing and lean on the jamb.

"If she was so obsessed with him," I said, "that she bought his house and dug up his cellar, and came to spend random days and weekends here, absorbing his vibes, why didn't she just move here and get a job in Manhattan? Somebody with her talents and her CV? Any firm in Manhattan would snap her up. How did she know there was a body down there? Who told her? Did she buy this house, not for Allan, but because she was searching for that body?"

She let me finish and said, "I found some photo albums. Thing is, the vinyls on one side and the books on the other are covered in dust. But the albums are clean."

I felt a jolt of excitement. "Have you checked them?"

She smiled. "No, I thought you'd like to share the task."

I nodded. "Let's go."

We clattered down the stairs, back to the living room. On the coffee table at the center of the nest of white leather armchairs and sofa was a stack of five crimson photograph albums, each spotlessly clean, as though they had been recently wiped.

I sat on the sofa and took the top album. Dehan sat next to me and took the next. I didn't open it but examined it carefully, then opened it and examined the plastic sheets that held the photographs in place. I looked at Dehan.

"These albums are as old as everything else here. I'd stake my life on it. This album, at least, is from the eighties." I looked down at the first page of photographs. "As old as these pictures."

There were pictures of a tall, dark-haired man. He was handsome, and there was something charismatic about him. His hair was long, unfashionably so for the '80s, and his clothes—flared jeans, sweatshirts, and aviators—were more '70s than '80s.

In most of the pictures he was with a woman whom I recognized as Marie, and a small female child I figured was Rachel, the eldest of the sisters. They were pictured by a swimming pool somewhere in the country, on a beach which might have been in Florida, riding horses somewhere very green with tall pines.

Increasingly, as I turned the pages, Allan's appearance became more unkempt. There was a wild air about him and his clothes. His wife and daughter were always immaculate. They looked expensively dressed, with class if not always elegance. But he appeared in cutoff jeans, unhemmed, bare-chested, with ever longer hair and a beard.

And as his aspect changed, so Jay Petrov and Hal Mahoney appeared more frequently in the pictures, along with an increasing variety of other people, mostly young, student types—and mostly girls.

Dehan reached the end of the album she was looking at and snapped it closed.

"It's corroborative of what we already know."

I nodded, sucking my teeth and staring at the last photograph in the album I had in my hands.

"The point is, somebody was interested enough in these albums to wipe the dust off them and sit and look at them regularly. Two gets you twenty that somebody was April Olsen. Let's face it, there is no trace of anybody else in this house until a couple of nights ago."

I was looking at a large print of a barbeque in what appeared to be the backyard of the house. There were a lot of people, and a lot of bottles and glasses. Everybody seemed to be either laughing or drinking. Marie was not there. I spotted Hal Mahoney and several others who seemed to show up regularly, but Jay was absent too. I wondered if he had taken the photograph. Allan was at the center, sitting sideways on a table. He had a young girl on his lap, and they were both pretending to suck on a huge joint at the same time. For a moment I had the strange impression that it was April Olsen sitting on his lap. I tapped the girl and showed the picture to Dehan. She frowned hard, and then I heard a sharp intake of breath.

"Holy shit!"

"It's not my imagination, is it?"

"No!"

"That's May Olsen, April's mother. She said she'd never met him."

"Maybe it was a one-off, Stone. Is she in any of the others?"

We took another album each and trawled through them. It was not a one-off. It was not a single party she had been to and then forgotten about. There must have been twenty or thirty pictures of them together. In some they were just hanging out, in others they were embracing, in still others they were kissing passionately.

Dehan dropped her album on the table, open on the last page.

"They were having a goddamned affair, Stone! They were lovers."

"We should have seen this from the start."

"How? How could we have?"

I looked at her and smiled. "The same way April did." A thought came to me. "Wait a minute. What was May Olsen's single name?" A stab of anger made me swear. "Goddamn it! Dehan, it's in the damned file! How could we have missed it? May Olsen née Rose. Her single name, the name she was registered at college under, was Rose! Jay Petrov told us, Bernstein had hooked up with a girl called Rose. He called her Rosie. It was May Rose! God*damn* it!"

Dehan puffed out her cheeks. "Holy shit! That was not an easy connection to make, Stone. She hid it well."

"Yeah, April knew her mother was dishonest, a fraud. Just like we did the moment we walked through that door into that office.

Lying comes as naturally to the Olsens as eating, breathing, and making bank deposits."

"I guess you're right. But where the hell does this leave us?"

"It may begin to explain April's obsession, and why she was so desperate to find Allan."

She frowned. "It does?"

I nodded. "Yeah. She believed he was her father."

Her eyebrows went high, and she leaned forward, staring at me. "Say *what*?"

"It probably started with that feeling all teens get from time to time. She saw herself as different to the rest of the family, like she didn't belong. Only as time passed, what started as a feeling began to be confirmed. She *was* different. She was mentally more free, a bit more wild, anarchic, whatever. Her mother said it, she was more like her."

"She did say that."

"Simon—well, we've both seen Simon. He's Mommy's precious boy and does exactly what he is told. And as for Geoffrey, he is everything that Simon will become. I guess April took after her mother, but she didn't see it that way. I don't know what it was, Dehan, maybe she saw a photograph, or she caught a careless comment from her mother, but she began to recognize herself in the stories about Bernstein. And at some point I guess she did the math. She was born roughly nine months after Bernstein left for Mexico. She became convinced he was her father, and believed all her wildness and that fierce, unfettered intelligence came from him. And I think she may have been right."

"That is one hell of a leap, Stone. And if it's true, which I am not saying it is, how the hell'd she find out?"

"My guess? When we confront May with this she'll tell us that she and April had a heart-to-heart when April was sixteen or seventeen. Like I said, Dehan, it probably started with May telling some funny stories about Bernstein. He must have had a hell of an impact on her. She probably talked about him often. April became interested and one thing led to another."

Dehan flopped back in her chair. "Jeez! It's kind of depressingly predictable. She had an affair with Allan because he was charismatic, the bad boy par excellence, but after the fun and games, he got serious and so did she. But where he got serious about her, she got serious about her career. She had probably recently met Geoffrey and knew he was the stone on which she was going to build her career. Allan went to pieces, went to New Mexico, and started writing conciliatory letters to his ex-wife. When she brushed him off, he went to Mexico, shacked up with some Mexican chick, and peyoted his brains out."

I took a deep breath and let it out noisily.

"Apart from the fact that you just turned peyote into a verb, I think you may have nailed it. But and however, Little Grasshopper, none of that acute insight explains, A, who is the man in the shallow grave, B, what caused April to get murdered, or C, how she and the man in the shallow grave came to be shot with the same revolver."

We sat in silence for a moment as I went through the photographs again. After a moment she looked at me with eyes that were two thin slits.

"I disagree."

I was surprised and told her so.

"I think," she said, "that what it does is give substance to the theory we already had. April was obsessed with finding the man she thought was her dad. She connected with Petrov, her dad's best friend, and he added fuel to the fire of her belief and her fantasy, because he could get inside her pants. They went to Mexico together, searching for him." Now she raised an index finger. "Then one of two things happened. Either they found him or they didn't."

I smiled. "Can't argue with that."

"Assume they did. Our theory that either Bernstein or Bernstein and Petrov killed that guy and buried him still holds strong. In a moment of indiscretion either they both tell her, one of them tells her, or she overhears them talking about the murder and the body. One way or another she discovers they killed this guy. She comes back to New York with Petrov—or with both of them—and she digs up the body. She confronts them with what she has found, and they kill her, using the same gun they used to kill the guy in the grave. Which raises the possibility that the gun belongs to Bernstein and he carries it with him."

I turned it around in my head, looking at it from every angle.

"It's a good working hypothesis."

"Jeez, boss! Give me a second to fan myself before I swoon and fall down."

"We really need to find out who this guy is in the shallow grave."

She made a face, pulling down the corners of her mouth.

"Let's go ask Jay Petrov."

I gave my head a little shake.

"No. I'd rather ask Allan Bernstein. In fact, I'd like to ask them both at the same time, but in separate interrogation rooms."

"That would work. Petrov would go to pieces like a plate of Jell-O on a kettle drum."

I tapped the albums. "Nobody knows we have these. Let's keep it that way for now. Let's go to the chief, tell him we need to go look for Bernstein, persuade him to approve a visit to Turicachi. Meanwhile, we get the DC police to haul May Olsen in so we can tell her we know about her and Bernstein. But we don't tell her how we know. I want to see which way she jumps. You never know, she might just know who John Doe is and where Bernstein's holed up."

Dehan gave her head a little sideways jerk. "It's a long shot, but she might."

I echoed her gesture. "Not so long. They had some pretty wild parties, and if these photographs are anything to go by, she was at most of them right up to the end. If you're right and there was some kind of Charles Manson crap developing, that might just have been the thing that made her jump ship and seek the safer, less crazy waters where Geoffrey Olsen navigated."

She frowned with her eyes closed. "Sorry, I got lost in your maritime metaphors. Are you saying that Bernstein's ever crazier parties might have spooked her because they started playing with the idea of killing somebody?"

"That's what I am saying. If things were getting that crazy, it might have sent her running into Geoffrey's secure and sensible arms. It might just be that she knows who that guy is."

"Yeah, that is definitely possible."

"I want to scare her." I thought a little longer. "We tell her we have a witness who places her at the parties as Bernstein's girl. Bernstein and his pals had selected somebody to sacrifice, and the witness says May knew who the victim was going to be. We tell her we have the witness in the next room spilling his guts. I want to see how she reacts."

"Before we go to Mexico . . . ?"

"Yeah, before we go. We have no idea how much she knows. Hell! For all we know she might still be in touch with him. I mean, the question remains. If Jay is telling the truth and they never found Bernstein, how the hell did April know there was a corpse down there?"

"So wait. This is an alternate theory. Are you saying maybe May knew and told her?"

"Somebody did. Logic dictates it was either Bernstein himself, Petrov, or May. Now it turns out Bernstein and May were lovers, in this very house. If May was at that party, and she was Bernstein's lover, there is every chance she was a witness to the killing and knew where the body was. We said before, that may have been the very thing that made her break up with him. Now think, there was a lot of conflict between May and her daughter, and it all centered around this house and Allan Bernstein. If May wanted to scare April off Bernstein once and for all, what better way than telling her the very thing that made *her*, May, stop seeing him?"

"That Bernstein had killed somebody and buried him in the house."

"Exactly. If we can, we should try and crack her before we go galloping off to Mexico."

"Ten-four, big guy." She leaned forward and patted the albums. "Let's get these bagged up and over to the lab."

"Agreed. And then, finally, the chief."

She winked at me and grinned. "Woohoo! Road trip!"

THIRTEEN

THE CHIEF WAS AT HIS BONSAI AGAIN, FEEDING IT FROM his tiny green watering can. Dehan closed the door behind us, and I frowned at the diminutive plant.

"You know it won't grow, don't you, sir?"

He beamed at me happily.

"Well, that's it, you see? It's a bonsai. They are miniature trees, from Japan. This one is a plum tree, but it will never grow to its full size because the roots have been trimmed." He gazed at his tree a moment, smiling, muttered, "Japanese . . ." then returned to his desk and bid us be seated.

"The April Olsen, John Doe case," he said.

"Yes, sir. There have been developments, and we need to make two requests."

His mouth and his pencil moustache beamed, but his eyes thought they'd hang around a bit and see what it was we wanted.

"Two?" he said. "I have no doubt, coming from you two, they are sound. Tell me."

I took a breath, organizing my thoughts, and sketched out our original conversations with May, Geoffrey, and Simon Olsen, in DC and in New York. Then Dehan sketched in what Petrov and

Mahoney had told us about Bernstein's increasingly wild behavior and his disappearance to Mexico. He listened carefully, with his fingertips resting on the end of his desk in front of him.

"None of it made much sense," I said, finally, "but we went to have another look at the house. We hadn't had a chance yet to go over it carefully, and we both had a feeling it had more to tell us. We weren't wrong, sir. Dehan found a stack of photograph albums. Their condition, compared with the rest of the living room, showed they had been viewed recently. When we examined them we found some thirty photographs showing May Olsen and Allan Bernstein in a very intimate relationship. This would have been around the time that she was a student at Columbia, just before he went to Mexico." I spread my hands. "Like I said, sir, May Olsen had told us she had never met Bernstein."

His eyebrows went high on his forehead. "Oh, indeed . . ."

"We have a working theory, sir, that the unidentified body in the grave was somebody they killed during one of their parties. It was the express purpose of their parties to expand and alter their states of consciousness. We all know that often that just means losing all your inhibitions. This guy's death may have been part of an exercise in self-liberation, a sacrifice, or maybe things just got out of hand. Either way, we think May Olsen was a witness to the murder and knew the body was there. And we think April found out, either through Jay Petrov, Bernstein himself, or through her mother, and that's why she dug it up."

"So . . ." He paused, staring at his fingertips, which were still laid out on the edge of the desk. "So, either she went to Mexico with Professor Jay Petrov and found Bernstein, and they told her about the body, or she went with him and didn't find Bernstein, and her mother, on discovering that April was searching for her father, attempted to put her off by telling her about the body."

"Exactly, sir."

"And the first thing you want from me is to liaise with the DC police and ask them to bring in May Olsen and hand her into our custody as a material witness to John Doe's murder, and possibly her own daughter's too."

"Yes, sir. I think it would also be prudent to bring in Jay Petrov."

"On what grounds?"

"He may have informed April about the body, if her mother didn't, and he was almost certainly a witness."

"Can you prove that?"

"To a high degree of probability. In all the photographs where Bernstein appears with May Olsen, Petrov is there. He also had a long-term relationship with April, and they both searched for Allan Bernstein together in Mexico. He claims they never found him, but we are not convinced. Amongst other things, John Doe and April Olsen were both shot with the same revolver, thirty-five years apart. Chances are high that that revolver belonged to Bernstein, so there is an even chance that it was Bernstein who killed April. That being the case, it is likely they found him."

He frowned. "It's possible. Not a certainty, by any means, but it is possible."

"I have a hunch, sir, that April believed she was Bernstein's daughter. If she persuaded him to come back to New York with her, after searching for him for so many years, and revealed that she had found the body . . ."

"Yes, yes . . ." He sighed noisily and glanced at his bonsai. "It is a very compelling theory, but very thin on actual evidence and facts . . ."

"That's why we need to pull in May and Petrov . . ." I drew breath and added, "And go to Mexico."

He actually laughed. It wasn't a big roar of laughter. It was more like a small giggle, followed by more arched eyebrows and another, "Oh . . ."

Dehan spoke up. "If Bernstein is in Mexico, sir, we really need to bring him back."

"Yes, oh, indeed! But there are procedures for these things. We contact the Mexican police . . ."

"With all due respect, sir. That has already been tried, and it has yielded no results. Not because he isn't there, but because it is a very remote area of Sonora where what little law enforcement there is doesn't give a damn about some gringo living out in the desert on a diet of peyote and Coronitas."

He sighed. "I understand. But you must also understand that I cannot authorize you to go into a foreign jurisdiction—it's not even another state, but another country!—to carry out an arrest."

I laid my hand on Dehan's arm before she could answer.

"No, sir. We don't want to arrest him, or do anything that would violate Mexican sovereignty or their jurisdiction. We just want to go there and ask him some questions, and maybe try to convince him to do the right thing, morally, by coming home to testify."

He sighed again. "You mean you want to kidnap him."

"Not at all, sir. We just want to fly to Phoenix, drive down to Turicachi, which is a few hours' drive, locate Bernstein, talk to him, get his testimony, and come home." I hunched my shoulders. "Now, if Dehan went on her own, I don't know what to tell you. She'd probably bring back Bernstein and half the Sinaloa Cartel too. But I expect to act as a moderating influence on her, sir." I saw him falter and added, "It is absolutely true, sir, that the Mexican authorities either cannot or will not help us, but Bernstein is essential to this investigation. It's the price of a couple of airfares and a car hire. A couple of days or three."

He took a deep breath.

"I have absolute confidence in both of you. Otherwise I would not dream of authorizing this. Officially you are on leave, visiting Mexico. You are absolutely *not* authorized to undertake any kind of criminal investigation in a foreign jurisdiction. Do *not* . . ."—and here he looked directly at Dehan—". . . cause an international incident."

She muttered, "Of course not, sir. We are very grateful."

"You know what total deniability is?"

I nodded. "Yes, sir."

"Well, I am invoking it here." He puffed out his cheeks. "So, how do you want to arrange this? You want to go to Mexico first and then pull in Olsen and Petrov . . . ?"

Dehan shook her head, and I said, "No. We need to pull her in now. We'll book the flights for tomorrow, but I want May Olsen and Jay Petrov in custody by this afternoon."

He nodded. "Fine, I'll have your tickets booked for tomorrow afternoon. Meantime you go fetch Professor Petrov and I'll talk to the DC police. I hope you understand that we are treading a very fine line here, John."

I told him I understood, and we went down to get the car. As I unlocked it, Dehan leaned on the roof in the sunshine and called Columbia University.

"Yeah, good morning, this is Detective Carmen Dehan of the New York Police Department. Can you tell me if Professor Jay Petrov has come in yet this morning?"

There was a brief silence, and then Dehan made a listening face and blinked a few times.

"Okay, thanks." She hung up and looked at me. "He's not answering his phone in his office, and nobody has seen him yet. After our chat over breakfast he probably took a pill and went back to bed."

I pulled open the door. "Let's go see."

But five minutes of ringing and hammering at Professor Jay Petrov's door provided us with nothing to see but a closed door and a silent house. So Dehan called in and put out a BOLO on him while I got hold of his wife's telephone number and called.

"Professor Margaret Petrov?"

"Speaking."

"We met earlier this morning. My name is Detective John Stone . . ."

"How could I forget? You ruined my breakfast. Breakfast is very important to me, you know."

There was a certain amount of humor in her voice, and I

feared she was going to tell me I owed her breakfast, so I cut it short.

"I am sorry about that, Professor. Do you happen to know where your husband is right now?"

"I assume he's at work."

"He's not at the university and he's not at home. We need to talk to him."

"Have you tried his cell?" And then, with a different tone of voice, "What is this about, Detective?"

"I haven't got his cell number, Professor. We need to talk to him. We believe he may be a material witness in at least one homicide."

I heard the sharp intake of breath. "You can't be serious! *Jay?*"

"Yes, I am very serious. Can you give me his cell number?"

"No, *wait*! What are you talking about? How can *Jay* be a material witness in a *murder*? This is ridiculous!"

"Professor, if you believe we are impersonating officers of the law . . ."

"No! Look! Just give me a moment to adjust, will you? Just explain . . . *How* is Jay a material witness in . . ." She gave a short, humorless laugh. ". . . in *at least* one homicide."

I paused a moment, then asked her, "Were you acquainted with Professor Allan Bernstein?"

"No, I heard about him . . ."

"Were you aware that your husband was an intimate friend of his?"

"Yes . . ." Then, "Oh, God . . ."

"We need to talk to your husband urgently. I am not saying that he was involved in the murder, Professor, but he may have been a vital witness to what happened. We need to talk to him. We also need a description of his car and his license plate."

"Oh, God . . . Fine, I'll WhatsApp you his number and the details of his car. Will you please let me know when you have . . ."

Her voice faltered, and I knew she was crying.

"Of course."

I hung up. Dehan said, "You think he's done a runner?"

"I don't know. I guess it depends how deeply involved he was. What did they tell you at the university?"

"He hasn't shown up. They'll contact us when he does."

I walked to the car and drummed my fists gently on the roof. Dehan watched me and asked, "What do we do?"

I spoke to the leaves in the trees above my head.

"I don't know yet."

A moment later my cell pinged. It was the WhatsApp from Margaret Petrov. I gave Dehan the details of the car, and she updated the BOLO, wandering up and down the sidewalk. Meanwhile I called Petrov's number. It rang for thirty seconds.

"This is Professor Jay Petrov. I may be busy, or I may just be relaxing, reading a book, or doing any number of things that are not your concern..."

I hung up. "His answering service."

"Son of a bitch has gone to Mexico to warn Bernstein."

I glanced at her but didn't answer. She pulled her cell from her pocket and stabbed at the screen, then put it to her ear.

"Yeah, Dehan." She gave her badge number. "I need a trace on a GPS... a cell phone." She looked at me. "What's the number?"

I gave it to her. After a moment she said, "Yeah, Professor Jay Petrov. I need to know where he is." She waited a moment, then said, "Sure, I'll wait." She hung up. "She'll call me back. Two gets you twenty he's at JFK."

I drummed some more on the roof. She glanced at me twice and asked me, "Why aren't you saying anything?"

I shrugged with my eyebrows and shook my head. "Because I have no idea what's going on. I am waiting for some kind of illumination."

"You're kidding, right?"

"No."

"We alerted him this morning and he got the hell out of Dodge."

I grunted.

"What?"

"It doesn't explain everything."

"Like what?"

I hesitated, spread my hands, and turned to lean my ass on the hood and look at her.

"The letters."

"*What?*"

"The letters, Dehan. I told you, those letters are the key. But this does not explain those letters."

Her face screwed up like a confused fist. "*Stone!* We came here this morning, told him we had caught him in a lie about his and Bernstein's relationship with the victim, and now he's gone. How much clearer do you want it?"

"There's something else."

"*What?*"

"Don't get exasperated, Dehan. It was something Simon said, repeating something April had said to him."

She frowned and said again, more quietly, "What?"

"That she had said to him she had bought the house because she wanted to be close to Bernstein. That he was, quote, 'one of the great thinkers of the twentieth century,' and, above all, 'she wanted to have the house that he had inhabited, so that she could be close to him.'"

She gave her head several rapid shakes and shrugged. It was a very Latin gesture.

"So what? I don't get what you're driving at."

I drew breath to answer, but her phone rang. She stabbed the screen and put it to her ear, staring at me.

"Yeah, Dehan." She remained silent a moment, then, "Can you double-check that please? We are actually . . ." More silence while her face grew madder. I sighed. I knew what she was going to tell me because, somehow, that did make sense. She said, "Yeah, okay, thanks," and hung up. She pointed at Petrov's house. "The phone is in there. It *might* be in one of the neighbors' houses, but you and I both know it's in there. He's dumped it and taken a burner."

I called Margaret Petrov again. Her voice sounded weary.

"Yes, Detective. I have tried Jay's phone several times. He is not answering."

"I know that, Professor. Your husband's telephone is inside your house. We are going to need either your permission or a court order to get inside and see what is going on."

"What do you mean, 'what's going on'?"

I heard I had a call waiting.

"Your husband has not gone to work today. We confronted him with some very serious news this morning about a homicide in which he may be involved. Do I need to spell it out for you? We need to get inside, Professor."

The call-waiting went away, and a moment later Dehan's phone rang. Margaret Petrov said, "Oh, dear Lord . . . No, no, you don't need to spell it out. I'm on my way."

"Professor, where is your au pair?"

"She has the rest of the day off. Why?"

"Because I need to get into your house, now. Do I have your permission to force the lock?"

She was silent while the meaning of my words sunk in.

"Yes," she said at last. "Yes, of course."

I hung up. Dehan was listening to her phone, staring at me. Finally she said, "Yes, sir. Thank you, sir."

She hung up. "Tickets are booked for tomorrow afternoon. He's spoken to the DC police. They have a BOLO out for May Olsen and they are sending a patrol to her house and her office. They'll let us know as soon as they have her in custody."

I nodded once. "Margaret Petrov is on her way. We have permission to go in."

Dehan sighed noisily. "We're wasting time. He's either at JFK or he's in a car headed south."

"There are BOLOs out on him and his car."

"Yeah, I guess." She turned, and I followed her toward the

door. "So what were you saying?" she asked me. "I don't get it. She bought the house to be close to him, and she thought he was one of the great thinkers. So what?" She waited a moment, then added, "We spooked Petrov and he ran. Period."

"Yeah," I said, with not much enthusiasm as I pulled my Swiss Army knife from my pocket and rammed it in the lock. "Period."

FOURTEEN

The house was very silent. The entrance hall was shaded and cool. Dark, mahogany stairs ascended to the upper floors on the right, and at the bottom of the stairs large, walnut doors stood ajar onto what I guessed was a living room. A luminous patch of red carpet shone through, where the sun lay stretched across it. On the left was the passage we had followed earlier to get to the conservatory and the kitchen. Opposite the living-room door, another door stood closed.

I clicked on Petrov's number. After a second it began to ring in the living room. Dehan pulled on her latex gloves and stepped forward. I said, "Dehan."

She turned. "What?"

"Call Columbia. Ask if Hal Mahoney went in today." She stared at me as I moved toward the living-room door, with its luminous patch of red carpet. I said quietly, "I'm going to call Dispatch."

She didn't answer. I nudged the door open and stood looking as I pulled on my own gloves.

Tall, old pine bookcases, raw gray, not varnished blond. A superabundance of books stacked wherever and however. A wrought iron fireplace between two alcoves, each stacked with books. A bow window overlooking Henry Street. A bright red carpet, probably Wilton, wall to wall. Huge armchairs and a huge sofa, not matching and not a recognizable designer. A heavy wooden coffee table, smothered with magazines, two newspapers, and several books, pressed open so as not to lose the place, eloquent of curiosity without respect.

Over on the left, French windows onto a lawn, closed. A bigger fireplace, marble, and a huge, rustic table, also gray pine. More bookshelves, more books, and a marble-topped dresser facing the fireplace across the table. Candles in expensive French wine bottles, and beside the nearest one, a cell phone, black, sleek.

I hung up.

In the doorway I could hear Dehan saying, "He hasn't been in either? Okay . . . yeah, do that. Thanks." To me she said, "He hasn't been in."

I pressed the number for Dispatch. When they answered, I identified myself and told them, "I need a car to go to the home of Professor Hal Mahoney of Columbia University to check he is safe. I haven't got his address. They need to find it fast and get there straightaway. Do it now. The unit may need backup."

I hung up. Dehan spoke to me from the door.

"What the hell's with you, Stone?" I pointed at the phone on the dresser. She said, "Like I said, he left his phone and ran. He's probably bought a burner . . ."

I slipped past her back into the hall. "Maybe you're right. Take a look in that room there, will you?"

I pointed to the closed door across the hall as I climbed the steps. I heard her voice behind me, tinged with sarcasm.

"Sure thing, boss."

I was on the first landing, with another just above me. There was a bathroom on my far right, and two bedrooms directly in front, both closed. I had a quick look in the bathroom, saw nothing out of place, and opened the door to the first bedroom.

The limp posters on the wall, the small desk, and the half-empty miniature bookcase said it had once been occupied by a child. Either that or it was still, occasionally, occupied by a child. The drapes were closed, and narrow beams of light lingered in the dark air where vertical shafts of floating dust intersected them.

I closed the door and moved to the next room. Here the windows overlooked the backyard and the lawn. The drapes were also drawn closed, but slits of green light shimmered between the curtains, and in the slight glow they cast I could make out a freestanding wooden wardrobe, two chests of drawers, and a very large brass bed with bedside tables to either side.

Jay Petrov was lying on the bed with his back to me. There was a glass on the bedside table nearest me. It looked and smelled like Scotch. Across the bed I could see another. There was also an ashtray, a small, wooden cask, some screwed-up tinfoil, and a rollup burned out in the ashtray. The boiled-cabbage smell of marijuana was powerful.

I heard Dehan's feet on the stairs, and a moment later I felt her presence by my side.

"Son of a gun!" she said. "He was here all along, getting stoned!"

I didn't move.

"He wasn't alone." I pointed to the ashtray and the second glass. I glanced at her. She was frowning. I said, "So I'm wondering where his friend is and, above all, why he is still dressed."

"Shit . . ."

"You want to check the kitchen? But do me a favor, have your piece in your hand."

She nodded but jerked her head at Jay. "Check."

I moved around the bed, saw the pallid, gray skin of his face, and knew he was dead. I felt for a pulse in his neck to confirm it but knew I wouldn't find one. I looked at Dehan and shook my head.

She pulled her piece and said, "I'll call it in."

As she trotted down the stairs I could hear her on the phone, asking for backup, a meat wagon, the ME, and the crime scene team. Meanwhile I searched for an immediate cause of death. I couldn't find one. He hadn't been shot with a .38, that much was clear. There was no foaming at the lips, no strange smells; his eyes were closed and peaceful, his physical posture as though he had been sleeping.

I examined the room carefully, searching for anything that was out of place or out of the ordinary in the bedroom of a mature married couple. I found nothing. The only thing that was odd or out of place was the dead body lying on the bed. So I stood, at the foot of the bed, rested my ass on the chest of drawers, and stared at that body on the bed for a while. Eventually Dehan appeared at the doorway again.

"Clear downstairs. I checked upstairs too."

"There is nothing out of place . . ." I gestured at the bedside tables. "Except whiskey in the morning, for two, and the joint." I squinted at her through the gloom. "What was that room on the left? A study?"

"Yeah."

"Did it have a French window?"

"Yeah."

"It was open?"

She looked surprised and repeated, with some emphasis, "Yeah!"

I grunted and sighed. "Well, we'll see what Joe can find on the glass."

"And the joint," she said. "The paper should have the killer's DNA."

I made a "maybe" face. "Mixed in with his. If it's there."

She frowned. "You knew he was here, didn't you?"

"It was a growing possibility. How do you think he died?"

"It was a growing possibility? Not for me it wasn't! You should have told me."

"You wouldn't have believed me. You would have asked me, 'What's with you, Stone?'" I made a fair imitation of her voice and chuckled. "How do you think he died, Dehan?"

She tore a resentful gaze away from me and turned it on the dead Petrov, then moved around to hunker down and look into his face.

"He wasn't shot. He wasn't strangled. No smell of bitter almonds, no frothing. Unlikely to be poison, unless it was curare." She glanced at me. "In the whiskey?"

I made a "maybe" face.

She said, "Is curare from Mexico?"

"I don't think so. As far as I know it's from South America. We'll have to wait till Frank gets here."

She stood and wandered around, looking at the body from every angle.

"Right now it looks as though he just . . . *died*."

I stared around the room again, trying to find any indication of the killer's presence apart from the whiskey and the joint. I couldn't see any.

"If it was poison," I said, "it's a fair assumption that it was administered either via the joint or the whiskey. So presumably traces will be found. I just don't get why the killer made no effort to remove them."

We didn't get much further, and after ten minutes we began to hear the approaching sirens. The patrol cars arrived first and set up a perimeter. Shortly after that Frank arrived, with Joe and his crime scene team just behind. Dehan went down to meet them and came back with Frank. Joe and his team were still suiting up downstairs. He glanced at me and then at the body. I said, "We'll get out of your way in just a moment, Frank, and let you do your job. I'm just curious. There appears to be no obvious cause of death. Dehan suggested curare . . ."

"It's much too soon," he said absently, and advanced to the bed. He inspected the back of Petrov's neck, speaking half to himself. "Sometimes an ice pick or similar to the base of the skull, but nothing like that here . . ."

He moved around the bed to inspect Petrov's face. Dehan

said, "Is there any Mexican equivalent of curare? Something a Mexican shaman would know about?"

He stared at her a moment, then returned his gaze to Petrov's gray face.

"Erythrina," he said, fingering open the lifeless eyes. "Known there as *zompantil*. Very widely available in Mexico. The bark and stem have similar properties to curare, and the seeds have been used in Mexico for centuries to kill animals. The plant contains a mixture of isomeric alkaloids called erythroidines, all of which produce similar effects to those of the curare alkaloids, binding to the active sites of receptors at the neuromuscular junction and blocking nerve impulses from being sent to the skeletal muscles, effectively paralyzing them and bringing about death by asphyxia, while the heart continues beating and the victim remains horribly conscious, unable to cry out or move." He looked over at me, then at Dehan by the door. "You think that's what killed this man?"

I shrugged. "That's probably putting it a bit strong. But there is no obvious cause of death." I gestured at the glasses and the paraphernalia for the marijuana. "He was obviously accompanied, and ingesting . . ."

He grunted and after a moment looked at us both again like he was surprised we were still there.

"You said something about going away and letting me do my job . . . ?"

Dehan regarded me with hooded eyes. "I love Frank. He's such a sweet guy."

I pushed off the chest of drawers and joined her at the door.

"That's because you don't know him. Under that sweet exterior he is all meanness and bad attitude. Let's take a look around the house."

We didn't get far. As we headed for the second flight up to the upper floors, the sound of raised voices and a woman shouting came to us from the front door. Dehan stopped and leaned over the banister.

"I think the other Professor Petrov just arrived."

Dehan went down ahead of me because she was younger and more agile and could take the steps two at a time. When I got to the front door, Dehan was joining a group of two uniforms and a sergeant who were trying not to get into a row with Professor Margaret Petrov. Dehan started to tell her to take it easy, which made Margaret Petrov's freckled face turn crimson.

"What are you *talking about*? How can I take it easy when I get home and find my *goddamn house full of policemen*?" She waved her hand wildly at the ME's car and the crime scene van and added, "*And the damned medical examiner!*"

I spoke with just enough volume to be heard and snapped, "Let her through!"

She liked that and pushed through the small crowd, making straight for me. I held out both hands to take her shoulders and spoke very firmly.

"You are right to be concerned and distressed, Professor Petrov." She stopped, and I took hold of her shoulders and squeezed. "I have some very bad news for you. I am afraid your husband is dead, and it seems he may well have been murdered."

I watched her carefully: her skin tone, the size of her pupils, and her breathing. She might have faked it, but if she did, she had a degree of control over her autonomic system which was almost superhuman. Her face drained of blood, her pupils became pinpricks, and her breathing became irregular gasps of breath. She shook her head in a small burst of rapid shakes.

"No! No! *No!*"

I put my arm around her, and Dehan closed in on the other side. Between us we guided her up the steps of the brownstone and into the living room, where we sat her on the sofa. She stared into Dehan's face. Her mouth was an ugly, sagging gash of red. She gripped her hand and turned her face to me.

"What on Earth? This can't be true..."

Dehan stood. "I'm going to see if Frank has anything for her."

I nodded, and Dehan left, taking the stairs three at a time. I took Margaret Petrov's hand in both of mine.

"Professor, I know from personal experience how hard this is. But even so, I am going to ask you to try and answer just a couple of questions for me. Because in a moment the doctor is going to sedate you and then you won't be able to answer me. Do you understand?"

She nodded. I pulled a handkerchief from my pocket and handed it to her, because the full impact of the reality was sinking in, and tears were flooding from her eyes and spilling down her face. She covered her mouth with the handkerchief, searching my face with her eyes.

"But, where is he? Why can't I see him? What's happened?" She shook her head. "This doesn't make any sense."

"He's upstairs, and I need you to think hard about this morning. Did he do anything, say anything, anything at all, that struck you as out of the ordinary?"

"Well, *you arrived*!"

"Yes, that's true." I nodded. "But aside from that, did he receive a phone call? Did anybody contact him? Was he expecting anybody?"

She froze. Her gaze went past me to the wall, and she became abstracted.

"Yes, but it wasn't today. It was last night, in the evening. He received a call."

"Did he say who from?"

She gave her head a small shake, still abstracted, staring at the wall.

"No, he wouldn't tell me."

"Did he say anything at all about the call, or the caller?"

"He said an old friend was coming to see him, and he would be staying at home this morning. He and the friend had things to talk about." She finally looked at me again. "Old times, he said."

I squeezed her hand. "Think very hard, did he say anything at all that might suggest it was either a man or a woman? Did he refer to 'him' or 'her,' 'he' or 'she'?"

"I . . ." She closed her eyes. "I really can't be sure . . . After your visit, I just assumed it was Allan."

Frank's voice came from the door behind me.

"That will be quite enough, John. You can grill her tomorrow. Right now this poor lady is going to rest."

She watched Frank roll up her sleeve, insert the needle, and slowly press down the plunger. She blinked a few times, then looked up at me and at Dehan. Her lip curled, and the tears began to spill again. Her voice, when it came, was a plea.

She said, "Where is he?" and she sank back against the sofa and closed her eyes.

FIFTEEN

"So this son of a bitch is still in New York."

Dehan was sitting on the hood of my Jag, with dappled sunlight playing across her face and her jeans, through the leaves of the pin oak and the London plane trees overhead. I didn't answer her, and she went on.

"And he's working his way through everybody who can finger him for the murder thirty-five years ago. April alerted him, and now he's making his way through the people who witnessed it."

I chewed my lip while I nodded, then sucked my teeth while I stared at the foliage overhead.

"Funny way to kill, isn't it?" She stared at me from her burgundy seat on the hood of my car. I stared back and said, "He shoots April in the chest, in an almost exact reenactment of John Doe's murder thirty-five years earlier, with the same weapon. Then he comes to his old pal's house and slips him a dose of erythrina, or whatever it was, in his whiskey, in the bedroom."

She looked away, down the road, then looked back at me with a touch of defiance in her face.

"Old times," she said, and shrugged. "The joint, the whiskey. Jay said their relationship was not homosexual, but it might have been bisexual . . ."

I made a kind of wince. "Allan Bernstein is in his eighties, Dehan. And from what I have seen, Petrov's taste ran to pretty, young, feminine blondes."

"Goddamn it, Stone!" She looked away, down the street again. "What, then?" She turned back. "I mean, you know the old Holmes thing, right? You taught it to me. 'Eliminate the impossible and whatever is left, however improbable . . .'"

"Is the truth. I know."

"Well, we are running out of impossibles, Stone. Besides, thirty-five years living in the Mexican desert can make you pretty tough, even at eighty-something."

"That's true enough. But we face a more immediate problem. Is there any point in going to look for him in Mexico if he is here in New York?"

"I know. That's what I was thinking." Her face contracted suddenly with irritation. "What the hell are they playing at in DC? Why haven't they pulled in May Olsen?"

I took a deep breath and heaved a heavy sigh.

"If your theory is right . . ."

"Don't say that, Stone. It's right. You know it is."

"Okay, fine, that being the case, May Olsen is our prime witness and also *his* prime target."

"I know." Her voice was heavy. "So what do we do now?"

I considered her face and was quietly astonished, not for the first or last time, at how beautiful she was, and how fortunate I was. I smiled at her, and she smiled back, a little quizzical.

"We go to Mexico, according to plan," I said.

"But . . ."

I interrupted her by shaking my head.

"No. There is nothing we can do here right now. We put out a BOLO on Allan Bernstein and we take May Olsen into protective custody. We're not just looking for Bernstein, Dehan. We are looking for any evidence that he was ever there."

"Of course he was there!"

"Is that what we're going to tell the jury?"

She closed her eyes, calling on her patience. "Fine. No. We need to prove it."

"That's right, Little Grasshopper. And there is something else too."

"What?" She was frowning, like she didn't trust me. "What other thing?"

"You remember Marie Bernstein?"

"Yeah, of course."

"Do you ever stop and wonder about what happened to her?"

Her brow creased. She said, tentatively, "No . . ."

"I do."

"Like what?"

I gave a big shrug and a big sigh at the same time.

"What did Jay Petrov tell us about her?"

"Jeez, Stone! Now? Let me try and remember . . ."

I nodded. "I'll be right back. I just want to check something out."

I went inside and found Joe with Frank upstairs.

"What can I do for you, John?"

"I need Petrov's DNA compared with a sample I sent you the other day."

I told him which one, and he and Frank both stared at me a moment. Then Frank said, "Oh, that's deep. That's very deep."

Joe said, "I've got ANDE in the van. I'll run a sample now and make a comparison. I'll have it in the hour."

"Thanks, Joe. While you're at it, I'd like you to run another comparison. You already have the profiles. I just need them compared."

I told them which ones, and Frank scratched his head.

"But, what would that mean?"

"That's what I was wondering."

I went back down and found Dehan still sitting on the hood. I said, "You're sulking. Good girls don't sulk."

"Why are you asking me to think about Jay Petrov and Marie Bernstein?"

"I don't know, Dehan. Because I think we have been coming at this all wrong. I told you, the key to this whole thing lies in those two letters, and what made him wait seventeen days before going in search of his shaman. When you start thinking about that, about those letters, about the *content* of those letters, and above all what is *not* in them, other possibilities begin to emerge."

She shook her head. "You lost me. I don't know what you're talking about. I'm going to call the station and see if there's any news from Washington."

"While you're at it ask if they found Hal Mahoney."

There wasn't, and they hadn't, and she hung up, pushed her ass off the hood, and stuffed her hands in her jeans pockets.

"There is no point in going to Mexico if he is here!"

"Dehan—"

"What?"

She turned to glare at me. I said, "If Allan Bernstein did this, he is no longer in New York."

"Why?"

I sighed. "Open questions, Dehan. Try closing it up a bit."

She rolled her eyes. "Okay! What would make him leave, or prevent him from staying?" She nodded and spread her hands. "Okay, you're right, that's more focused. So, uh, he'd want to get the hell out of Dodge." She was thinking, spreading her hands wide as ideas came to her. "There are, as far as we know, no more important witnesses here, so he is going to move on . . ."

"And where will he go?"

"Okay, he'll either go to DC to hunt down May, or he'll head back home to Mexico."

"That is my thinking, Dehan, with the small exception that I believe there is one other witness in New York."

"Hal Mahoney."

"Yes. But we have a BOLO out on him too, we have a BOLO out on May Olsen, and we have a BOLO out on Bernstein. There is nothing we can do here right now until we can prove either that

Bernstein has been living in Mexico for the past thirty-five years, or that he has not."

She sagged slightly. "Yeah, okay."

I went on. "Now, we can leave it to Border Control to pick him up as he tries to reenter Mexico, but what description do we give them, after he's been living in a shack in the desert for the last thirty-odd years?"

"Yeah, yeah, okay, you made your point."

"So, right now, it seems to me that the best use of our time and energy is in Mexico. Unless..."

"Unless what?"

"Unless you want me to go to Mexico and you wait here and interview May Olsen when they bring her in."

She thought about it. "Would that be better?"

"It might be. Wait."

I took out my cell and called Simon Olsen.

"Olsen speaking."

"Mr. Olsen, this is Detective Stone."

"Oh, yes, what can I do for you? The police have been asking..."

He trailed off, but I wasn't listening.

"Mr. Olsen, when was the last time you saw your mother?"

"Why, um, last evening. The local police have been asking the same question. Would you mind telling me what is going on? I must say you are causing a frightful fuss."

"She might be at risk, Mr. Olsen, and we need to talk to her. If you know where she is..."

"What are you talking about, at risk? That's absurd!"

"About as absurd as her daughter getting murdered?" I heard a sharp intake of breath. "You need to think before you speak, Mr. Olsen. We have reason to believe that whoever killed April has killed again and may now be after your mother. If you or your father have any idea where she is, you need to tell us."

"I told the local police and I am telling you the same thing. I have no idea where she is. She should be in her office. I have tried calling her, but her telephone is switched off."

"What about your father?"

"He is convalescing, and I will not have him worried by this."

"The moment you hear from her, Mr. Olsen, you let us know, and the DC police."

"I have been told this already, Detective Stone."

"But apparently you had not been told that she was at risk, or that a close friend of hers had been murdered this morning."

He didn't say anything for a long moment. Then he spoke quietly. "No, I hadn't been told that. But now I have, and you may be sure that I will contact you the moment I hear from her."

I thanked him and hung up. I stood staring at Dehan.

The clatter and rattle of a gurney made me turn. Two paramedics were working their way down the nine stone steps of the stoop. They reached the bottom, and I watched them roll the covered body across the sidewalk toward the ambulance. They opened the back and began to maneuver the gurney into it. Frank emerged from the house and trotted down the steps. He stopped beside me. Dehan was watching him sullenly.

"Before you ask," he said, "time of death is between when you last saw him this morning and when you found him; so sometime this morning. Cause of death is as yet impossible to say, until I open him up . . ."

A thought suddenly nudged to the front of my mind, and I hollered at the guy holding the back of the gurney.

"Wait! Hold up!"

He looked surprised, and I walked over. Frank and Dehan followed close behind.

The front of the gurney was in the back of the ambulance, but the rear wheels were still on the blacktop. I pulled back the blanket and said to the paramedics, "Help me turn him on his side."

Frank pushed forward, his face flushed.

"Now hang on just one minute!"

"I'm not going to spoil your body, Frank. I know what I'm doing. I need to see something. Now help me turn him on his side."

He didn't like it, but Frank and the paramedics helped me roll Petrov on his right side, so he had his back to me. I pulled on my latex gloves again and very carefully lifted his sweatshirt until it was just above his sixth intercostals. Frank and Dehan came around to have a look.

Frank's face was screwed up with concentration. "What the hell are you doing, Stone?"

I peered a little closer, pulled my cell from my pocket, selected the magnifier app, and moved slowly across the area.

"There!"

My finger appeared huge on the screen just above what looked like a small freckle. Frank said, "It's a . . ."

I interrupted. "It's a puncture. You're going to find a fine needle wedged in there, between the ribs, maybe a hatpin or something like that, snapped off on the outside. It has penetrated through to the heart, and he has died of internal hemorrhaging."

Frank was shaking his head. "How could you possibly know that?"

Dehan echoed him: "How could you know . . . ?"

I clicked the screen to capture the image, then stood. "It was the only thing that made sense," I said.

Dehan's jaw actually sagged a couple of inches.

"That makes sense?"

"Yeah," I said, offering her a smile. "Perfect sense."

Frank gestured at the paramedics to lay the body down again.

"Enough parlor tricks, John. I'll have a report for you as soon as I can . . ."

"Yesterday is soon enough, Frank."

"I can't go any faster than I can go, even if Carmen were to ask me." He walked away toward his car. "I'll be in touch."

We watched the ambulance pull away, followed by Frank's sedan.

"So." Dehan screwed her eyes up at me. "You going to explain?"

"There's not a lot to explain, Dehan. It just makes more sense. The killer arranged the meeting late yesterday afternoon. That's how they knew Margaret would be at work, Maria would have the day off, and they'd be alone with plenty of time to carry out the kill without being disturbed. It seemed to me the objective was to kill him in the bedroom, stage it as though he'd been having an affair, and leave before Maria or Margaret got home. It also had to be a quiet kill, hence the absence of a .45 revolver." I shrugged. "All that made sense, but the erythrina, curare thing didn't, not in that context. The poison had to be put in his drink, and the drinks were poured downstairs. You noticed there was no bottle up in the bedroom, so the glasses had been carried up from the living room, along with the paraphernalia for the joint. That meant they had been drinking downstairs, so the killer could not be sure of where the poison was going to take effect. He could have dropped dead halfway up the stairs, or in the living room, and the effect would have been spoiled.

"Much more predictable, and easier to control, was a needle through the fifth and sixth ribs, straight into the heart, and then snap off the end. It's held firm by the ribs, while the heart tears itself to shreds on it and the victim dies a swift death by internal bleeding. And the two great advantages are that the wound is all but invisible, and it can be administered during an embrace."

"What?"

I advanced toward Dehan and made as though to take her in my arms.

"I hold you, and I have the pin or the needle in my sleeve. As I take you in my arms, I calculate the position of the intercostals, and ram the needle home between the ribs. Once the ribs have gone into spasm and clamped onto the needle, I can snap it off, and you are effectively dead. I lay you on the bed, arrange you as though you are sleeping, and go."

She was still frowning hard. "Okay, but then what about the

whiskey glasses and the joint? What is the point of staging a love scene, and why leave all the evidence?"

"You can bet the killer never touched any of that. We'll know tomorrow for sure, but two gets you twenty the only thing the killer ever touched was Petrov. The killer obviously knows Petrov's reputation and staged it so the killer could be any one of a number of jealous lovers. What the killer did not know was that we would be here."

"How could you *possibly* . . ."

I shrugged. "One thing makes sense, so you move on to the next logical inference. It was not logical, if the killer had gone there for the purpose of killing him, as they most certainly must have, that they should carelessly smother a joint and a glass of whiskey with their DNA. Neither did it make sense that the killer, having left their prints and DNA, should leave those glasses and the joint there on leaving. The only possible causes of death, seeing him as he was, were that he had either been poisoned or stabbed with a long needle. The poison was out, so it was a needle."

"I could never do that—be that sure of a line of abstract reasoning like that."

"But I wasn't sure," I said. "That's why I went to check."

"Oh," she said flatly. "Okay."

I patted her shoulder. "Come on, kiddo. Let's go prepare for Mexico."

We still hadn't heard from Hal.

SIXTEEN

Everything was scorched. As far as you could see in any direction, everything was scorched, dry, in shades of gray, ochre, and rust. The hills on our right were dotted with skinny, stunted trees that struggled against desiccated earth and a leaden, molten sun to suck what life they could out of the dry soil and the scorched air.

We passed a green sign that told us we had arrived at Turicachi. Beyond the sign there were scattered shacks, hovels, and caravans with improvised porches made of sticks, poles, and blankets: anything to keep the sun away and make some shade. We cruised past them, followed by incurious eyes—eyes that would have been curious if they hadn't been sapped of all vitality by the relentless, unforgiving sun.

We passed a cute bandstand, which was probably the best-constructed building in the village, surrounded by four white benches and eight nineteenth-century lampposts, also painted white. There were few houses as such. There were improvised dwellings composed partly of brick, partly of wood, and partly of corrugated sheets of asbestos.

Then, on the right, we came to a broad esplanade. Like everything else it was composed of baked dust, and where the hot breeze was drawn into spirals, ghosts seemed to rise up and drift, aimless, across the open ground.

I slowed and turned in. Forty yards from the road there was a large shack with a Coca-Cola sign outside, and above that another sign that announced this was the Imperial Supermarket, it had air-conditioning, ice-cold drinks, and, not only that, but ice too.

We rolled up to the door in our rented Cherokee, killed the engine, and climbed out. Dehan stepped onto the wooden porch and pushed through the door ahead of me into the cool, air-conditioned shade. A bell chimed and chimed again as I followed her in. There was a bead curtain behind the counter. Through it emerged a woman who looked like a Turkish wrestler's armpit. She stood and watched us with small, mildly outraged eyes, eyes that became sharp and suspicious when Dehan spoke to her in Spanish.

"*Déme dos cervezas frías.*"

The woman rolled away to a freezer and came back with two bottles of Sol, which she placed on the counter in front of us. Her eyes narrowed, and she spoke with defiance.

"*Tres pesos!*"

Dehan gave me a glancing smile and snapped, "*Ábralos!*"

The woman scowled and cracked the bottle on an opener she had screwed to the inside of the counter. I was thirsty. I grabbed one of the bottles and took a long pull while Dehan extracted a one hundred peso note from her wallet and showed it to the woman.

"*Me lo puede cambiar?*"

She was asking her if she could give her change. She had a smile on her face that said she knew she couldn't. The woman looked nervous. She shook her head. Dehan turned to me. "She says she can't change it."

I shrugged and drained the bottle.

Dehan took a swig, and as she set down the bottle she said, "*Quizás tenemos que comprar otra cosa.*" She turned to me again. "Maybe we need to buy something else, right?"

I nodded. "Sure. How about some information?"

"*Por ejemplo, información?*"

The woman swallowed hard. "*Que información?*"

Dehan leaned on the counter and looked the small woman in the eye.

"*Un Americano, nombre de Allan, que vive aquí en el desierto. Buscaba un brujo para aprender sobre peyote y ayahuasca. Usted le conoce?*"

I had no idea what she'd said, but I caught the key words: Allan, desert, brujo, peyote, and ayahuasca. The woman stared her in the eye so long I thought she'd been transfixed. Then she glanced down at the bill, swallowed again, and shook her head.

"*No.*"

Dehan pulled out another C-note and said, "*Usted sabe algo. Dígamelo.*"

The bead curtain rattled, and a very small man with a straw hat and a blue gingham shirt pushed through. He looked old enough to have hunted mammoths in his teens. He had the remains of very white hair, and very blue eyes. He scowled at me but kept the best of it for Dehan.

"What you want, fuckin' gringos?"

Dehan offered him a smile that was more amused than friendly.

"No need for that, pal. We are just trying to find an old friend." She raised the two bills to show him. "And we're willing to pay for any help you can give us."

He made a face like he'd bitten into a lemon.

"What *frien*?"

I stepped up, put my empty bottle on the counter, and took the bills from Dehan's fingers. I folded them and put them in my wallet, holding the small guy's eye while I did it.

"His name is Allan. He's tall, like me. Today he is maybe late seventies or eighty years old. He's crazy. He needs help. He likes peyote and ayahuasca. He came here years ago looking for a brujo. Do you know who he is?"

He jerked his chin at my chest.

"And the money?"

"Well, now, you be polite and tell me where we can find our friend, and then you get your money. But you keep on with the bad attitude, amigo, and things will be different. Do you know him, yes or no?"

He stared at me a long time with no expression. Expressionless staring was obviously the big thing with this guy. I sighed and turned to Dehan. "We're wasting our time. Let's get out of here."

I turned and heard the woman squawk. As I reached for the door, the guy said, "Wait, *un momento*, maybe I can tell you something."

I turned, with my hand still on the handle. Dehan said, "Make it good, old man, I'm losing patience."

"I don't know your frien' Allan. Bot, out in the desert there is a brujo. He makes medicine with peyote and ayahuasca. A lot of people go to him when they got problem. He is real old. Maybe your frien' went to him. Can we have the money now?"

"It's a big desert. Where in the desert?"

"You gonna go south." He pointed south toward the wall of his shop. "Ontil you come to a long buildin' with a playground for the kids. There you gonna turn right, cross the railway lines, and you gonna follow the road, pass the fields, ontil you come to the trees. Then you gonna turn north, right, okay? And you gonna go up into the hills, followin' the track." He shrugged. "If he don't want you to find him, you ain't gonna find him. If he want you to find him, you gonna find him."

I pulled out my wallet and handed over two hundred pesos, a grand total of nine bucks. He snatched them from my hand.

"You no tell nobody we tol' you, huh? El Brujo is real dangerous!"

Dehan shook her head. "Don't worry, old man. We won't tell nobody."

We stepped out into the scorching sunshine and clambered

back into the Jeep. I fired up the big engine, and we pulled out of the lot. Dehan was smiling.

"You got real badass in there, big guy. I thought you were going to tell him to make your day."

"That would have been impressive if he hadn't been four foot three and nine hundred years old. What do you make of it?"

She sighed as we cruised south on the blacktop.

"I don't know, Stone. The letters were posted from Esqueda. Esqueda has two hotels, our Esmeralda and the Hotel Esqueda. Nobody in either of them has ever heard of Allan Bernstein, by name or description. Same story at the post office. But they all know about El Brujo." She was silent for a moment as we passed the schoolyard and turned right to bounce over the railway tracks. Then we were on a broad track of beaten earth, heading out of town toward the desert and the distant hills. I drew breath, and she started talking again.

"If they know El Brujo, why the hell don't they know Allan? Okay, so it was thirty-five years ago, and if all that time he has been living in the desert cooking his brains in peyote juice, maybe they all forgot about him. But it's hard to imagine Allan Bernstein keeping that quiet for a third of a century. The guy was all about noise, showing off, upsetting people, causing controversy . . . How come nobody knows he's here?"

I negotiated a couple of bends, and pretty soon we were out in the desert, headed south and west, trailing a huge cloud of gray dust. I said, "Don't forget . . ."

She pointed at me. "I was just going to say, don't forget how scared the old guy at the shop was."

"That's what I was going to . . ."

"Now, if Allan became El Brujo's pupil, and people began to think of him as El Brujo as well . . . like there are now two El Brujos . . ."

"I get it. That's what I was going to . . ."

"And maybe Allan spread the word. 'If anybody comes asking for me, you never heard of me.'" I didn't answer, and she grinned, leaning her back against the door, with the desert sliding past in her aviators. "Is that what you were going to say?"

"Yup."

"So how old do you figure El Brujo was thirty-five years ago?"

"I don't know, but pretty old I guess."

"Say he was sixty."

"We have no evidence for that."

"Now he'd be ninety-five. If he was seventy, now he'd be a hundred and five."

"And if he was a two-year-old prodigy today he'd be thirty-seven. I know what you're driving at, Dehan, but we don't know."

She ignored me and rolled on.

"So the guy we are going out to the desert to meet could actually be Allan Bernstein. El Brujo died ten years ago, and he is El Brujo's heir. And that is what April and Petrov found when they got out here. He swore them to silence . . ."

"But?"

She was quiet, staring out at the empty, lifeless landscape sliding past in hues of gray and red.

"They wanted him to go home. He refused. He'd probably finally driven himself crazy. April insisted, and Petrov, perhaps growing jealous, blurted out that Bernstein could never go home, because of the murder."

She paused and shifted in her seat to face me.

"After they left, he couldn't settle, going crazy thinking about how April would go to the cops, or tell Marie what had happened. He became paranoid. So he cleaned himself up and took the trip to New York to tie up his loose ends."

I made a face that was skeptical and showed it to her. "It's a great story, Dehan. But it's the theory we already had, only now Bernstein has become a shaman. You have to admit it sounds a little improbable."

She narrowed her eyes and wagged a finger at me.

"Eliminate the impossible . . ."

"I know! I know!"

"... and whatever is left..."

"Yeah, I know."

"... *however improbable* ..."

"Yes!"

"... is the truth."

"Yes, Dehan, I know. But have we eliminated the impossible?"

She snorted. "So far, Sensei, just about everything seems impossible, except what I just suggested."

I shrugged but didn't answer, and we rattled and rolled along for another ten or fifteen minutes with her staring at me. Eventually she pushed her shades up on her head, like a medieval visor, and said, "Son of a gun."

"What?"

"You think you've cracked it."

"No, I don't."

"You do. You think you cracked it back in New York, at Petrov's house, when he was murdered."

I shook my head.

"Nah."

"Nah? You never say 'nah.'"

"Dehan, seriously, I maybe had a few thoughts..."

"Son of a gun. You went back into the house. You went back into Petrov's house. What did you do in the house?"

I laughed, then shook my head in a way that might have been a little patronizing.

"No, I just had a word with Frank and Joe . . . Look! The trees. What did he say, turn right here?"

She didn't answer, but I slowed where the road split into a fork and turned right. After that we began to climb slowly through sparse woodland and sand.

"Has it occurred to you, Dehan..."

"Probably not."

"Don't sulk. Has it occurred to you that identity is a bit of a recurring issue in this case?"

She thought about it for a moment, then shrugged. "Not really."

"I mean, it starts about thirty-five years ago, when John Doe gets buried in Bernstein's cellar. Nobody, at least in New York, reports him missing. Who is he? Nobody knows. Now, thirty-five years later a girl is killed in the same place with the same weapon, having dug him up. She was easy to identify, but, I believe she herself did not know who she was. And that is why she was searching for the man she believed was her father. And finally, Bernstein, April, and Petrov were all searching for the nameless brujo, who may in the end turn out to be Bernstein himself. Identities, Dehan. This is a fog of identities. Nobody knows who anybody is."

"Why are you telling me this?"

"DNA."

"What?"

"DNA. Thank heavens for DNA. I went into the house because I wanted Frank to do a little cross-referencing of DNA, to see if I could get a clearer picture of who was whom in this muddle." I pointed through the grimy windshield. "What's that?"

I pressed the lever and squirted water over the windshield, which the wipers mixed with the dust and made a thick layer of mud. I slowed to a crawl and kept squirting until the mud cleared and we began to see more clearly.

Dehan said, "Stop," and pushed open the door. I came to a halt as she swung down, put the car in neutral, and climbed out. I joined Dehan at the front of the hood, and we stared up toward the top of a steep, barren hill on our right, peppered with rocks and boulders.

Barely visible near the top was a small patch of white against the ochre, red, and gray of the landscape.

"There." I put my arm around her and pointed. "See the speck of white?"

"It's a house, or a shack."

"How the hell do we get up there?"

"We follow the track for a mile. If we haven't found a right fork by then, we come back, find a copse where we can hide the car, and we climb."

"Sounds like a plan, kiddo."

So we climbed back into the Jeep and set off. I glanced at my watch. It was two p.m.

We rolled on for half a mile and, as Dehan had almost predicted, a rough track appeared on our right. I slowed right down and turned onto it, bumping and rolling over the loose rocks. Now the shack was more readily visible, with a terra-cotta gabled roof, whitewashed adobe walls, and a rough porch out front. It was maybe two or three hundred yards up the hill, and the path, such as it was, gradually became a goat track and then petered out altogether.

I reversed back onto the road, found the shade of some palo verde trees, and parked the Jeep. I grabbed a rucksack with a couple of liters of water, Dehan stuffed a cream suede Stetson on her head, and we began to climb.

SEVENTEEN

It took us a good fifteen minutes to clamber up the steep, bare hill, and by the time we reached the shack my legs were trembling, and we were both panting hard and sweating like horses.

As we had seen from the track, the adobe house was one story, with small, wooden-shuttered windows that were closed, and a roof made of corrugated tiles. The door, a mismatch of wooden planks painted blue, was half open. Dehan stood a moment leaning forward with her hands on her knees to catch her breath. I handed her a bottle of water. She took a drink, splashed some over her head and neck, and handed me back the bottle. After she'd wiped her face, she stepped over to the door and peered in. The contrast with the glare outside made the darkness almost impenetrable. She called out, "*Hola! Buenas tardes!*"

There was no reply. She glanced at me. "I'm a New York cop, right? I don't get spooked by empty houses. Right?"

I sighed, took a pull on the water, and poured some over my head. As I wiped it through my hair I said, "This may not even be the place."

"No," she said, and eased the door a little farther open. "This is the place."

She took a tentative step, then another, and I followed her into a dark room maybe twenty feet across and fifteen deep. The only light came from the thin, hazy shafts that angled in through the cracks in the wooden blinds, and the cracks in the ceiling. As my eyes grew accustomed to the dark, I saw that the floor was beaten earth, and there was a small, rudimentary fireplace on the left with a couple of iron pots and a wooden stool. On the right there was a mattress made of straw with a couple of Mexican blankets thrown over it. In the far wall there was another door, and hanging on a nail beside it was a straw hat. I pointed to it.

"If he went out, he didn't take his hat."

"In this heat?"

I stepped a little farther into the room. There was a faint smell of meat stew and aromatic herbs, and something else I couldn't identify.

I moved forward and pulled open the door. Glaring light poured in from an enclosed yard. It also had a floor of beaten earth, but the white walls were bordered with tiles which contained flower beds that were full of large, luxuriant, aromatic bushes: rosemary, thyme, sage, basil, and parsley were a few that I recognized. A rough wooden porch had been constructed over the door to give some shade. Dry branches covered the porch, and a vine had been trained over the top.

On the far right an annex had been built onto the house. This was painted terra-cotta, and the door was blue. There were no windows.

Dehan glanced at me. "You think he's in there?"

"Makes sense."

She called out again, "*Hola! Buenas tardes!*"

Again there was no reply. I walked up to the blue door and rapped on it with my knuckles. Still nothing. So I took hold of it and pulled it open.

The floor was of red clay. There were ashes in the center, where a small fire had burned. There was a man sitting beside it who was probably Mexican. I couldn't see his face because he was sitting cross-legged by the cold ashes, slumped forward, with what was left of his head in his lap. The back of his skull wasn't exactly missing, but it wasn't where it was supposed to be. It was lying all over the floor behind him, along with a good portion of his brains.

The hole in his head was swarming with flies, and the stench of decomposing flesh was overpowering. I covered my mouth with my sleeve and heard Dehan swear violently beside me.

She took a handkerchief from her pocket and spoke through it.

"Stone, we need to leave here right now! *Right now!* We need to turn around and get the hell out of Mexico! Now!"

"I know. But I need to do one thing first."

I stepped into the room and hunkered down among the splintered bone and gore that had exploded from the back of his skull. I reached in my jacket pocket and pulled out an evidence bag. I heard Dehan's voice, incredulous and exasperated at the same time.

"What the hell, Stone!" And then, "You brought *evidence bags*?"

I took my pen from my inside pocket and started sifting through the mess. I spoke absently, focusing on what I was doing.

"Yeah, I had an idea this might happen."

"Son of a *bitch*!"

"Here!" I made a scoop of the evidence bag and gently maneuvered the slug in. A little more sifting got me another slug, and into a separate bag I put as much organic matter and bone as I could find that seemed more or less clean. "Okay," I said. "Let's go."

"You know we are in deep shit, Stone. You know that, don't you?"

"If the authorities find us here, we will be in pretty deep trouble, Dehan. That is true. But it is equally possible that months will pass, and even years, without anybody ever finding this body."

We pushed out of his front door and began a half-running, half-stumbling descent of that steep hill, down toward the Jeep. As we went, Dehan spoke breathlessly over her shoulder.

"You keep thinking positive, big guy. Meantime, we need to get the hell out of here as fast as we can."

I slipped, stumbled, and fell, scrambled to my feet, and went after her again. She was saying, "I want to be out of Mexico *tonight*!"

"Ten-four!" I gasped and kept going.

We made the goat track and the going got easier. Then we were on the wider path and we were able to run more or less normally. We made the Cherokee a couple of minutes after that, and then we were clambering in, slamming doors, and gunning the engine. The tires spun, gripped the loose earth, and we were away.

We were doing forty, but it felt like we were doing a hundred and forty over the rough track. Dehan, gripping the door at the open window, said, "What exactly did you pick up?"

"Two slugs, and material for a DNA profile. I am pretty sure the slugs are .45s. I want to compare them with the slugs that killed John Doe and April Olsen."

She made a queasy expression. "And his brains?"

I glanced at her. "I want to know if he was Allan Bernstein."

"He looked pretty Mexican, Stone."

"Sure." I shrugged. "But in the photographs we saw he looks Mediterranean, olive complexion and dark hair. Put that guy in the desert for thirty-five years until he's eighty, and tell me you can distinguish him from an old Mexican shaman."

"Fair point. Jesus! When do we get to the blacktop?"

I slowed. "I don't want to go through that town like we're running."

I stopped and climbed out, poured water over the license plates, and threw a couple of handfuls of dirt at them. Then climbed back in and proceeded toward Turicachi and the main road.

We made it back to Esqueda by five p.m. On the way two police cars passed us going in the direction of Turicachi with their lights flashing and their sirens blaring. It might have been a drug bust. Sonora was becoming more dangerous as the drug trade was spilling over from Sinaloa. Or it might have been something else.

When we finally got there, I parked outside the Hotel Esmeralda on Agua Prieta-Nacozari De Garcia. It was a low building painted a sickly green color. The big porch over the sliding glass doors had corrugated tiles, hacienda style, but the actual roof of the hotel was made of sheets of corrugated steel. We stepped through the sliding glass doors, and Dehan climbed the stairs to our room to get our bags while I settled the bill.

The guy at the reception desk was about sixteen with a pencil moustache and black hair with enough oil in it to put OPEC out of business.

"You go so soon?" he asked. "I think you and the *señorita* gonna stay a few days to visit Sonora."

I raised an eyebrow at him as I handed over the money. "The *señorita* is my *señora*, and we decided to go and look at the Mayan ruins in Yucatan instead."

"Oh yeah, that's super cool."

I nodded at him like I was sure his opinion was important to somebody, but I wasn't that somebody, and turned to help Dehan with the bags. We slung them in the trunk of the Jeep and climbed in the cab, fired up the engine, and we were away. It's fifty miles from Esqueda to the border, and it's all the same road right from the door of the Hotel Esmeralda to Agua Prieta and Douglas. All I had to do was get behind the wheel, hit the gas, and go. And that was what I did, for five of those miles.

We were beginning to relax, discussing what condition the DNA might be in and whether Joe would be able to do anything with it, when I saw a wink of red and blue in my rearview mirror. I felt a hot pellet in my gut and said, "We have company."

She looked in the wing mirror.

"It may not be for us."

"Yeah, maybe not." I said it without conviction because I knew it was for us. "But if it is, who the hell told the cops to come after us? Is El Brujo's killer still here?"

I could now make out it was a Dodge RAM and it was moving fast, doing at least a hundred miles per hour. It drew up behind us, matched our speed, and stayed on our tail. In the mirror I could see there were two cops in the truck. I indicated right, that he could overtake, pulled into the side of the road, and slowed, to let him pass. But he didn't do that. What he did was pull up beside me, stab his finger at the side of the road, and shout, "Pull over! Pull over!"

I nodded, slowed more, and came to a stop by the side of the road. I glanced at Dehan. "Maybe they're just supplementing their income by preying on American tourists. Maybe we can bribe our way out of this."

The RAM pulled over in front of us, and the two cops got out and hitched their belts. They were both young, maybe in their early thirties. They both had black shades and both looked like they spent too much time in the gym. The one who was going to do the talking had a blond crew cut and German ancestors. The other was Latino. The Latino went and stood staring at our illegible license plate. The Aryan wonder came and peered in the window.

"Where are you going?"

I smiled. "Good afternoon, Officer. We're going back to the States."

"Where you comin' from?"

"We've been in Esqueda, driving around, doing some tour . . ."

He cut me short. "What were you doin' in Esqueda."

"Like I said, we . . ."

"Get out of the truck."

"Sure."

We climbed out, and the Latino took Dehan by the arm and pulled her around to stand next to me by the door. To his pal he said, "*La matricula es imposible de leer.*" The crew cut snapped, "Your license plate is so filthy you cannot read it! That is a violation!"

I nodded. "I'm sorry about that."

"What were you doing in Esqueda?"

"Like I said, tourism . . ."

"Lies! Name! Papers!"

I smiled at his pal and then at him. "So you are telling me you don't know my name?"

His face flushed red.

"I don't know your fockin' name, gringo! Now gimme your papers! Now!"

"You don't know my name, you can't read my license plate, and you haven't seen my papers . . ."

Nothing gets a little fascist in uniform madder than disobedience. He was real mad by now, and he was reaching for his piece to wave it in my face. I slid my right foot forward and, with a twitch of my hip, drove my right fist hard into the tip of his jaw, giving it the full benefit of my two hundred and twenty pounds. His eyes rolled up in his head, and he keeled over backward like timber.

Dehan and El Latino were both gaping at me, but I didn't give either of them time to process what I had done. I took a long step to my right and smashed the same fist into the same spot on his jaw. He went down in the same way. Dehan stared at them and then at me and said, "What . . . ?"

"Come on, we have no time. Help me get them into the patrol car!"

"What the hell have you done, Stone? You assaulted two police officers in a foreign . . ."

"I know what I've done, Dehan! Stop wasting time! Come on!"

I grabbed the Aryan dream's shoulders and she took his ankles and we carried him at a hobbling run back to the RAM. We slung him in the back with difficulty and tied his ankles and his wrists with his shoelaces. Then we used his shirt as a gag. We did the same thing with El Latino. Then Dehan climbed behind the wheel and drove the truck off the road, over the railway tracks, and tucked it behind a copse of palo verde trees.

Then she scrambled back to the Jeep, bringing with her their cells and their radios. She pulled the batteries, threw them on the back seat, and we burned rubber out of there.

We drove in silence for more than half an hour. Then Dehan turned in her seat and spoke.

"Stone, I cannot believe what you just did! Are you out of your mind?"

"Is that a rhetorical question?"

"Don't be a smart-ass, Stone! You just assaulted two cops in Mexico while we were investigating outside our jurisdiction. Do you remember that part of the conversation with the chief where he said, specifically, 'Don't cause an international incident'?"

"That *is* a rhetorical question. And besides, as I recall, he said that to you."

"Come on, Stone!"

I glanced at her. We were approaching an intersection just a mile outside the border town of Agua Prieta, by the San Bernardino River. I slowed and pulled into the roadside. There was nobody about, and the sky was getting that burnished look it gets just before the sun goes down.

"Dehan, those guys were looking for us. The very best thing that they had planned for us was to arrest us and chuck us in a cell in Esqueda. They would have our passports, our badges, the evidence bags, the hotel where we stayed—everything, and *then* we would have had an international incident that would have dragged in the chief, the precinct, the department, and even the damned White House. We had nothing to lose and everything to gain."

She screwed up her face. "What?"

"He told us, he couldn't read the plates, he didn't know our names, and he had not seen our papers. He'd just been told to look for a couple of Americans headed for the border, but he had no idea who we were. We had one chance and one chance alone of getting out of there without causing an international incident— and possibly with our lives. And that's what I did. Now, let's wipe the prints off these things and throw them off that bridge into the San Bernardino."

I pulled out again while she, sighing and shaking her head, took one of the phones and both of the radios, rubbed them clean, and, as we rolled over the bridge, hurled them far out over the side into the dark water. Then she took the remaining cell and typed a message to the sergeant at the Esqueda cop shop telling him where the dynamic duo were. Then that cell went into the river too.

We had no problems crossing the border and headed straight for Tucson, for some bison steak and some cold, cold beer.

EIGHTEEN

"So, here's the thing."

I was sitting on a chair in the bathroom holding a large glass of Irish whiskey while Dehan lay almost entirely covered in bubbles within the bathtub. Only her hands showed, her face, and the silky black knot on top of her head.

She spoke with her eyes closed.

"What thing?"

"Somebody knew we were there. Somebody knew what we were looking for, and that somebody bribed the cops to frame us for the murder of the brujo."

"That's an assumption, Stone. You don't know that."

"You're right. It's an assumption, but it's a pretty safe one. I'm not trying to sell this to a jury. I'm just trying to work out what happened."

"Okay," she said, still with her eyes closed.

"Now, in that heat, decay happens fast. You saw how many flies there were. And the gore from his brain was still moist. So even though Frank would throw his hands in the air in despair, I am going to go ahead and say the brujo had not been dead more than a couple of days, if that. So here are a couple of scenarios . . ."

I sipped my whiskey and stared at the ceiling for a moment.

"One, somebody back in New York called the sergeant at Esqueda a couple of days ago, when they learned that we were investigating the John Doe in Bernstein's cellar, and told him to go and eliminate either the brujo or Bernstein, depending on whether they are the same person or not. When that person discovered that we were going to Mexico to look for Bernstein, they called again and said, 'Stop these people from making it back to the U.S.A.'"

Now she opened her eyes and stared at me. "Jesus . . ."

I nodded at her. "I think that was a close call. The other possibility is that when that person, let's call them X for now, discovered we were going to Mexico to look for Bernstein, they called the sergeant and said, 'Go kill Bernstein, and then stop these two cops from getting back to the U.S.A.' There's not a lot in it."

She sat up with her elbows on her knees, the foam forming an alluring collar around her neck and chest, and frowned at me.

"Problems with your theory: first of all, it assumes the cops in Esqueda are corrupt, and we don't know that. Second, it turns our original theory on its head. Because we were working on the theory that Bernstein was our guy. Now Bernstein is being murdered. Who by?"

I shook my head. "We said from the start that there were probably witnesses to the murder . . ."

"And our prime candidate for that was Petrov, who is right now occupying a drawer at the morgue."

"Exactly, Dehan. Now keep going . . ."

Her eyes grew wide. "Son of a gun! There was a third guy in the trio. I keep forgetting him! Hal! Hal Mahoney. He was at least as devoted to Bernstein's ideas as Petrov was, and had an even worse attitude. The three of them were involved. They killed that poor guy and buried him. Bernstein went to Mexico to become a brujo, and Petrov and Mahoney withdrew from the crazy life and became eccentric professors. The whole thing gets forgotten, except that April becomes obsessed with the idea of Bernstein. Probably, as you said, she believed he was her father or something.

When she contacts Petrov, he seduces her, and they think they have her under control. He even takes her out to meet the great man himself. But when she goes and digs up the body, they then have a problem. So one of them, whichever one owns the original .45, shoots her."

I grunted. "We'll know more when we get the results from the lab. It should all be with Joe by tomorrow morning."

She scratched her nose and left a small cloud of bubbles there. "And when we tried to locate Hal," she said, as though she hadn't heard me, "he wasn't at work or at home, remember?"

I pulled my cell from my pocket and called the inspector at the 43rd. I told him we were back, in Tucson, and we'd be flying back to New York in the morning. I told him we'd gathered some forensic evidence, and he asked me not to fill him in on the phone, but to save it for the next day.

"Sir, before I hang up, did we get any hits on the BOLOs?"

"No, none. It's very peculiar."

"Yes, sir."

I thanked him and hung up. Then I called Joe at the lab.

"Stone, how was Mexico?"

"Productive, I think. I've sent you two slugs and a sample of brain tissue and skull. The body was at least a day old, and there were a lot of flies. I am really interested to know whether the two slugs match those that killed April and John Doe. But I am also very curious to know if this guy is Allan Bernstein."

"No problem on the slugs. But the DNA matching is complicated. Remember we ran Stella Bernstein's DNA against the John Doe in the cellar to see if he was her father, Allan?"

"Sure."

"We got a negative and concluded John Doe was not Bernstein."

"Right, yeah. I remember."

"And then, before you went off to Mexico, you asked me to do some cross-checking of the samples we had, plus DNA from Petrov. Well, I don't know where you got the inspiration from,

John, but Stella has quite a shock coming. Because Bernstein is not her father."

I snorted. "Petrov is. I was pretty sure of that. Stella's biological father is Jay Petrov. He and Marie had an affair when she discovered Bernstein was sleeping around with his pupils."

"I've asked Rachel for a sample . . ."

"You'll need to check it against the John Doe and the sample I've sent you."

"Sure, will do. When are you back?"

"Six p.m. tomorrow. What about the other test I asked for?"

"I haven't got there yet. I'll try and have something for you by tomorrow evening."

"Thanks, Joe."

I hung up and sat staring at Dehan. She stared back. After a moment she said, "That's what you went back in to ask him?" I nodded. She shook her head. "Why? Why would you do that?"

"Because of something Petrov said. He said that Marie didn't have what you would call an open mind, remember? He said her mind was narrow and closed, and when Bernstein started experimenting with hallucinogenic drugs, it really freaked her out. He said that after a while, he, Hal, and Allan would meet at Bernstein's place to conduct experiments, and Marie would leave. And then he said something that caught my attention. He said, 'At first I tried to help her. I tried to persuade her to stay and join in, but she didn't want to know. She was sweet, cute, but in the end she went running to Mommy every time we had a session.'"

"So?"

"'At first *I* tried to help her. *I* tried to persuade her to stay and join in,' not 'we tried.' Knowing Jay Petrov's weakness for women, and knowing what people can be like when they feel betrayed sexually, I got a hunch. I just had a feeling there was more behind those words than met the eye. Add to that the fact that Stella's age means she was conceived at right about the time Marie and Allan were breaking up . . ." I spread my hands. "It was a hunch, so I checked it out."

"So, what does it mean?"

"I'm not one hundred percent sure, but I think it means that the guy we found in Mexico was not Allan Bernstein."

WE TOUCHED down in New York at six p.m. the next day, collected the Jag from the parking lot, and headed straight for the 43rd. My cell started ringing as soon as we got out of the airport. I answered and put it on speaker.

"John, it's John. Did everything go all right in Mexico?"

I glanced at Dehan and smiled. "Nothing to report, sir, except that we picked up some material. It's with the lab right now. We'll tell you about it when we reach the station in about twenty minutes."

"Good, excellent, that's a relief. We've had some developments."

"What developments, sir?"

"May Olsen is in custody. It seems she and her husband were taking a few days off, recovering, at their country house in Virginia. When they were contacted by DC police they came voluntarily to New York, to the precinct."

Dehan made a face that said she was agreeably surprised. I said, "Anything else, sir? What about Hal Mahoney?"

"Still no sign of him. May Olsen posted bail. She and her husband are at their apartment on Riverside Drive, with the son."

"Good, okay. Sir, let's bring May in and have a talk with her. We're on our way from the airport right now. Sir, could you have them picked up, and bring Geoffrey and Simon along too?"

"I'll see to it."

When we got to the station, May hadn't arrived yet. I told the desk sergeant to put May in interview room three and to make Simon and Geoffrey comfortable wherever they could find space. Then I went to my desk while Dehan went to get coffee, and I called Joe at the lab.

"John," he said, "I was about to call you."

"I believe you. Have you got anything?"

"Yeah, the brain and skull material you sent in is not a match to anybody. But you were right about the other thing."

"How closely?"

"Close enough. No real doubts."

"Son of a gun. Thanks, Joe. I still owe you."

"Yeah. One day I'll collect. Then you'll be sorry."

I met Dehan outside the interrogation room, relieved her of one of the coffees, and pushed open the door. May Olsen looked up at us. She looked tired, and there was a hint of defiance and resentment in her eyes. I put a cup of coffee in front of her, and we sat.

"I wouldn't recommend drinking it. We've had it analyzed by the labs and even they don't know what it is."

She smiled and made it look sad.

"I am guessing you didn't bring me here to joke about bad coffee."

"You're right," I said. "I want to know, amongst other things, why you lied about not knowing Allan Bernstein."

She buried her face in her hands, and her voice came as a groan.

"I knew that son of a bitch would sink me one day, sooner or later."

We waited. Eventually her face emerged from her hands. It looked haggard.

"We met. I was a bad girl. I was always getting into trouble, but I knew—I thought I knew—I would always be able to get out of it. I lived by my own rules, and I was proud of it. Then I met Allan. He was handsome, ruthless, brilliant, and fascinating. What I didn't realize at the time I met him was that he was also driving himself into deep psychosis."

Dehan asked, "What kind of psychosis?"

"There is only one kind of psychosis, Detective, the one where you stop being able to tell the difference between your fantasies and reality. To me it was an affair. We played around with a few hallucinogens, had wild parties, wilder sex, and it was a gas."

I said, "But to him, the deeper he got, the more important your relationship became."

"Got it in one, Detective. He started getting into all this 'I was his yin and he was my yang' bullshit. We were paired souls, two halves of the same whole. He needed me to break through the portal into universal consciousness. It was fun when he spoke like that when we were stoned or high, but when he started talking like that when he was sober, it started freaking me out. It stopped being fun."

Dehan said, "Meanwhile, you'd met Geoffrey."

"Geoffrey was my salvation. He was solid, stable, hardworking, and had absolutely no interest in drugs or expanding his consciousness. So I told Allan we were through. And that was that. I made every effort to forget him, and that was the end of the story."

I leaned back in my chair and smiled. "That clears up a lot of question marks. I am very grateful. But there are still one or two points I am not clear on."

"Like what?"

"Well, you said just now that you made every effort to forget him, but that's not strictly true, is it?"

"What the hell are you talking about? Of course it is. I started a whole new life."

"If that's true, how did April discover that she was not Geoffrey's child, but Allan's?"

Her face went gray and pasty. She looked at the wall and licked her lips. "No, that's not . . ."

She didn't finish. She trailed off, and I started speaking again. "I know for a fact that she was Allan's child. And she knew it too. And there was only one way she could have known that, wasn't there?" She said nothing. "The only way she could have known that was if you had told her. How did that happen?"

"She was driving me crazy."

"It started with a funny story, right? A story about how crazy he was."

"We had some old friends over. They had known I was involved with Allan, and I had asked them not to talk about it, as Geoffrey was sensitive on the subject. But he went to bed and we had a few drinks, and the stories came out. Allan was insane. He did the most outrageous things . . . We had a laugh, remembered old times, and they left. But April, she was about fourteen, had been sitting on the stairs listening. She was fascinated by this man, and she kept pestering me about him. Who was he? Had I loved him? Why did I leave him for Geoffrey? April could never stand Geoffrey. In the end, when she was sixteen, I lost control and we had a furious screaming match and I told her that she was as crazy as he was, and she was his daughter. After that her obsession just grew and grew."

I said, "She bought his house."

"Yes. I wish Simon had told me about that. I think it started out as just wanting to be close to him. I think she wanted to find him, and she thought that there might be clues in the house as to where he had gone. She probably saw herself sifting through all his papers, discovering the material for an unpublished book, clues to where he was living . . ."

Dehan said, "Did you tell her about the body in the cellar?"

She seemed to drain to a paler shade of gray. Dark hollows showed under her eyes.

"What?"

Dehan smiled. "Come on, May. You must have known. You were there, at all the parties. You were his girl."

"What I'd like to know," I said, changing the subject, "is where the gun came from. I am figuring he bought it in New Mexico. He was becoming obsessed with death, wasn't he?"

She nodded. "Yes."

Dehan snapped, "He was beginning to talk about killing somebody. Is that right?"

"Yes."

Dehan drew breath, but I spoke first. "He went to New Mexico, trying peyote, and he came back with a .45 revolver, right?"

"Yes."

"And that was about the time you were getting ready to jump ship because he was getting out of control."

"Yes, that's right. I had the feeling he was getting dangerous, and I wanted no more to do with him."

"He went to New Mexico and did a couple of trips to Mexico too. Looking for this shaman, right?"

"Yes. He went a couple of times."

I reached in my slim card folder and pulled out the two photocopied letters I had picked up from my desk. Out of the corner of my eye I saw Dehan frown. I placed the letters in front of May and said, "And that was when he sent you these."

She shook her head. "No."

"He couldn't let go of you, and he kept writing to you to go and join him. You were his inspiration, his yin. He needed you to break through the portal. It's all there."

"No . . ."

"A lot of people don't know it, May, but paper is one of the best sources of fingerprints. They can last, undisturbed, for years. We have these, and the envelopes, at the lab right now. Whose prints do you think we'll find?"

"No, these were not to me. I have never seen . . ."

"Then it would be impossible for the lab to find your prints." I waited. She said nothing. I went on, "He sent these letters to you. When he returned from New Mexico he was raving, out of his mind. He was insisting, demanding that you go with him and help him in his research. But you were adamant that you were leaving him. What did he do, threaten you? Threaten Geoffrey?"

"He raped me, at gunpoint. When he was done, I knew I would never be free of him."

"So you shot him."

She closed her eyes, took a deep breath, remembered her training, and said, "I was in genuine fear of my life. I thought he was going to kill me."

Dehan was frowning, shaking her head. "So, you dug up the concrete?"

"No, he had already dug it up six months before. He wanted to experiment growing mushrooms down there. But he'd given up on that plan, and the sacks of cement were all down there. I spent that night burying him and mixing cement."

I picked up the story. "Then I figure you took his car, drove down to New Mexico, sent the first of those letters to Marie, and three weeks later you went to Mexico and sent the second one from Esqueda. If your daughter had not been so obsessed with her father, you might have got away with it."

She shook her head. "You never get away from something like that. It's with you always."

"You're probably right. Did you have to kill Jay Petrov?"

"Of course. He knew too much, about the parties and my relationship with Allan, and how bad it got at the end."

"Where is Hal?"

"At home, sleeping, like Jay."

I sighed, feeling suddenly weary. "What about that poor bastard in Mexico?"

"It was obvious, once you got onto Jay the whole thing with Mexico would unravel, and if you went and spoke to El Brujo you would know Allan had never been there. The next logical step would be that the man in the hole was Allan." She went quiet for a moment. "You observed once that we were not your run-of-the-mill human rights outfit. You were right. The clients we deal with are often Mexican and have a lot of connections. I made a phone call. I am surprised you made it back."

Dehan read her her rights, and a couple of minutes after that a sergeant came and led her away to a holding cell. When she was gone, Dehan sat staring at me.

"How didn't I see that? When did you see it? I still have a lot of questions, Stone . . ."

I nodded. "I'll answer what I can in a moment, Dehan." I leaned out of the door and asked a uniform to bring Simon Olsen.

While we were waiting, Dehan paced the room with her hands in her back pockets.

"I mean, what about April, for Christ's sake?"

Simon stepped in uncertainly, and the uniform closed the door behind him.

"What is this? Where is my mother?"

I pointed to a chair at the table and said, "Sit down. It's over, Simon. Your mother has confessed, and the best thing you can do is to do the same."

He sagged forward, covered his face, and started sobbing violently. I sat opposite him and spoke quietly.

"It was when she had come back from Mexico the last time, wasn't it? She no longer believed what Jay Petrov was telling her, about her father being in Mexico, living with a shaman. She was more and more convinced that her father was dead. She was smart, and it was a simple process of deduction. If he hadn't gone to Mexico, if she could find no trace of him anywhere, then he had never left New York. She knew how crazy things had gotten between her mother and Bernstein. What she hadn't got from May she had certainly got from Jay.

"Maybe we'll never know exactly what triggered it, but I figure it was the steady drip, drip of suspicion, and one day she got down in the cellar and dug a hole. Then I figure she called you. The same way she called you when she bought the house, and she invited you to have dinner in Greenwich Village. After dinner she told you to follow her home because she had something to show you. I figure she was drunk . . ."

He nodded. "She was drunk. And very emotional. She kept saying, 'Where is my dad?' and 'You have your dad, where's mine?' She was crazy, she dragged me from room to room, screaming at me, 'Where is my dad?'

"Finally she dragged me down to the cellar. I couldn't believe my eyes. She stood pointing into the hole at that horrible thing, and shrieking at me, 'There is my dad! There is my dad!' It was horrific."

I nodded like I understood and asked him, "Why did you take your mother's revolver with you?"

He was quiet for a long while. Finally he said, "Because I knew what she was going to show me. She had been talking about it since she'd got back from her last trip. She was convinced that Bernstein's body was in the house somewhere. When she called me, I could tell from her voice that she had found him. She said she was going to expose Mommy as a murderer, and when she showed me the horrible thing in the hole, I knew I could not allow Mommy and Daddy to be dragged into that and have their name soiled. So I shot her. And I left in a hurry."

"Did you tell your mother what you had done?"

He nodded silently, then said, "Yes, I had to tell Mommy, to make sure I had done the right thing."

"Of course," I said, "of course you did."

Then I read him his rights, and they took him away too.

EPILOGUE

We were sitting in the backyard, with all the lights off and only the dancing flames of the barbeque to illuminate us. The plates we had removed to one side, with what was left of the French fries, the salad, and the two large steaks. Dehan had brought out a bottle of tequila, and we were doing occasional shots and talking.

In answer to a question she had asked, I said, "First, like I told you, it was the letters. There was nothing in them to say he was writing to Marie. And the tone of the first one, the more I read it, the more it sounded to me like a letter to a lover. And the gap between one letter and the next, the only way I could make any sense of that was if it had not been sent by him, but by somebody else. Then the seed of the idea started to germinate. What if he had sent these letters to May, and May had simply stuck them in new envelopes, addressed them in capitals, and sent them to Marie, after Bernstein was dead. That would be proof that he had been alive and well in Mexico, after he was killed. It almost worked."

"So how did you know that it was him in the grave?"

"I didn't; it was a hunch until the last minute. I mean for one thing, the question kept nagging me: If his wife inherited everything, what was he living on? So I asked Joe to run John Doe's DNA against April's—they were practically a match. So John Doe was April's father, and had to be Bernstein."

"And May, in an effort to silence Jay, and knowing he was a sucker for a pretty woman, arranged to meet him when he was alone..."

I nodded. "A very dangerous woman. The kind of woman who uses a human rights practice to service the needs of drug dealers and the like. April was not wrong about her."

We knocked back two more shots. She smacked her lips and set down her glass.

"You know what I found real suggestive, Stone?"

"No, Dehan, I do not. But I hope you are going to tell me."

"I thought it was outrageous and scandalous the way you laid out those two cops in Mexico. But it was also *real* hot! And I think you should sling me over your shoulder right now and carry me upstairs."

So I did.

Don't miss IN HOT BLOOD. The riveting sequel in the Dead Cold Mystery series.

Scan the QR code below to purchase IN HOT BLOOD.

Or go to: righthouse.com/in-hot-blood

NOTE: flip to the very end to read an exclusive sneak peak...

DON'T MISS ANYTHING!

If you want to stay up to date on all new releases in this series, with this author, or with any of our new deals, you can do so by joining our newsletters below.

In addition, you will immediately gain access to our entire *Right House VIP Library,* which includes many riveting Mystery and Thriller novels for your enjoyment!

righthouse.com/email

(Easy to unsubscribe. No spam. Ever.)

ALSO BY BLAKE BANNER

Up to date books can be found at:
www.righthouse.com/blake-banner

ROGUE THRILLERS
Gates of Hell (Book 1)
Hell's Fury (Book 2)

ALEX MASON THRILLERS
Odin (Book 1)
Ice Cold Spy (Book 2)
Mason's Law (Book 3)
Assets and Liabilities (Book 4)
Russian Roulette (Book 5)
Executive Order (Book 6)
Dead Man Talking (Book 7)
All The King's Men (Book 8)
Flashpoint (Book 9)
Brotherhood of the Goat (Book 10)
Dead Hot (Book 11)
Blood on Megiddo (Book 12)
Son of Hell (Book 13)

HARRY BAUER THRILLER SERIES
Dead of Night (Book 1)
Dying Breath (Book 2)
The Einstaat Brief (Book 3)
Quantum Kill (Book 4)
Immortal Hate (Book 5)
The Silent Blade (Book 6)
LA: Wild Justice (Book 7)

Breath of Hell (Book 8)
Invisible Evil (Book 9)
The Shadow of Ukupacha (Book 10)
Sweet Razor Cut (Book 11)
Blood of the Innocent (Book 12)
Blood on Balthazar (Book 13)
Simple Kill (Book 14)
Riding The Devil (Book 15)
The Unavenged (Book 16)
The Devil's Vengeance (Book 17)
Bloody Retribution (Book 18)
Rogue Kill (Book 19)
Blood for Blood (Book 20)

DEAD COLD MYSTERY SERIES
An Ace and a Pair (Book 1)
Two Bare Arms (Book 2)
Garden of the Damned (Book 3)
Let Us Prey (Book 4)
The Sins of the Father (Book 5)
Strange and Sinister Path (Book 6)
The Heart to Kill (Book 7)
Unnatural Murder (Book 8)
Fire from Heaven (Book 9)
To Kill Upon A Kiss (Book 10)
Murder Most Scottish (Book 11)
The Butcher of Whitechapel (Book 12)
Little Dead Riding Hood (Book 13)
Trick or Treat (Book 14)
Blood Into Wine (Book 15)
Jack In The Box (Book 16)
The Fall Moon (Book 17)
Blood In Babylon (Book 18)
Death In Dexter (Book 19)
Mustang Sally (Book 20)

A Christmas Killing (Book 21)
Mommy's Little Killer (Book 22)
Bleed Out (Book 23)
Dead and Buried (Book 24)
In Hot Blood (Book 25)
Fallen Angels (Book 26)
Knife Edge (Book 27)
Along Came A Spider (Book 28)
Cold Blood (Book 29)
Curtain Call (Book 30)

THE OMEGA SERIES
Dawn of the Hunter (Book 1)
Double Edged Blade (Book 2)
The Storm (Book 3)
The Hand of War (Book 4)
A Harvest of Blood (Book 5)
To Rule in Hell (Book 6)
Kill: One (Book 7)
Powder Burn (Book 8)
Kill: Two (Book 9)
Unleashed (Book 10)
The Omicron Kill (Book 11)
9mm Justice (Book 12)
Kill: Four (Book 13)
Death In Freedom (Book 14)
Endgame (Book 15)

ABOUT US

Right House is an independent publisher created by authors for readers. We specialize in Action, Thriller, Mystery, and Crime novels.

If you enjoyed this novel, then there is a good chance you will like what else we have to offer! Please stay up to date by using any of the links below.

Join our mailing lists to stay up to date -->
righthouse.com/email
Visit our website --> righthouse.com
Contact us --> contact@righthouse.com

 facebook.com/righthousebooks
 x.com/righthousebooks
 instagram.com/righthousebooks

EXCLUSIVE SNEAK PEAK OF...

IN HOT BLOOD

CHAPTER 1

It had been raining for twenty-four hours solid. It wasn't cold, though. It was muggy. Sometimes the rain eased to a drizzle, but pretty soon it picked up again, swelled to a downpour, and then became torrential, drumming on roofs and cars and lashing wildly against windows. Sometimes it's nice to lie in bed and listen to the rain, especially if you're in good company; but not so much when it sounds like the world is coming to an end outside.

Dehan was asleep. She had that knack of being able to sleep wherever and whenever she wanted to, but lately she had been arriving home exhausted from her volunteer work, and she sparked out as soon as her head hit the pillow. All I could do was look at the reflected ripples and raindrops in the smoky, orange light on the ceiling and occasionally check the time.

Three o'clock in the morning. F. Scott Fitzgerald's words went through my mind: *In the real dark night of the soul, it's always three in the morning.*

I rose and went to look out the window. The road was flooded: a river turned copper by the streetlamps. The trees, jagged stencils against the water, bowed ponderously in the wind.

Twenty years earlier I would have smoked a cigarette at a time like this. I would have pulled a beer from the fridge, cracked it, and sat with the window open and my feet on the sill, smoking, drinking, and thinking.

Dehan stirred, and I turned to look at her. Long, brown limbs tangled in the white sheet, an ocean of black hair. My wife. For an instant I almost spoke, almost went to her to wake her, but the words died on my lips, and I turned back to the window.

When I grew tired of watching the spray, and the luminous interference patterns of the drops falling on the liquid copper river, I returned to the bed and lay staring at the ceiling again.

Four in the morning. Dehan was still asleep.

At five thirty I got up and went into the bathroom to shower. The bright light and the alternating hot and cold water cleared my head some. I stepped out of the shower, toweled myself dry, and went back to the dark bedroom with the orange streetlight reflected on the ceiling. Dehan was sitting up, on the edge of the bed, with her head in her hands. She looked up at me and smiled, sleepy.

"You're up early."

"I couldn't sleep."

She stood, put a hand on my shoulder, and kissed me on the cheek.

"How come?"

She didn't wait for an answer. She went into the bathroom and started brushing her teeth. I dressed and went down to make coffee.

She joined me about fifteen minutes later. Her expression was serious. She stood staring at me a moment. I had my ass against the sink, I was sipping coffee, and I had a piece of toast in my hand.

She said, "Are you having breakfast standing up?"

I shrugged. "We seem to have got into that habit."

A small contraction of her brows. "That's only while I'm working on the project, Stone."

I didn't answer, and she moved into the kitchen and started making pancakes. After a moment she stopped and turned to face me.

"It's six in the morning, Stone. We have time to sit down and have breakfast together."

I nodded, said, "Sure," and took the butter to the table. She watched me.

"You didn't tell me why you couldn't sleep."

"You were brushing your teeth and you wouldn't have heard me."

"Okay, what's going on?"

I didn't look at her when I answered.

"I wish I knew."

"What's that supposed to mean?"

"It means I don't know what's going on, but I wish I did."

"That's not helpful."

"Nope." Now I looked at her. "But it's the best I can do."

"You want to talk about it?"

My answer came out more bitter than I had intended. "Are you sure you have the time?"

She spread her hands in a gesture of helplessness and I went to get the maple syrup and a couple of plates. She was shaking her head.

"I don't believe it. You're mad because I'm involved in the project?"

"I'm not mad."

"You're sure acting like you're mad."

"I'm not mad," I repeated more deliberately, and then my mouth started talking on its own. "I just miss you. I miss having a wife. Instead of a wife I have a partner at work."

She sighed and sagged. "The kids really need this, Stone. It's a really important project..."

I nodded. "Sure. I guess it must be. It occupies all your free time, and lately that includes your days off. I see you at work and while you're asleep. When was the last time we had dinner together, at this table?" She didn't say anything, so I answered my own question. "Four weeks ago yesterday, a takeout pizza." I arched both my eyebrows. "I have a number of things I could ask that question about. When was the last time we—fill in the blank."

"I know, I know. There has been so much to do. It's hard to get volunteers, and Tony can't do it all by himself."

I was aware of a cold fire in my belly. I fought to control it.

"How long," I said quietly and deliberately, "is this going to continue?"

"Stone . . . !"

"I am not asking you to stop. If it means this much to you, then obviously you have to continue. I just want to know when, if ever, I am going to get my wife back."

"Of course you are! It's just . . ." She spread her hands again. "Another few weeks."

"Yeah, that's what you said three months ago. In fact, what you said was that you were volunteering for a month. Then it was a couple of weeks more, and then we just stopped communicating. I saw you at work, you stopped coming home for dinner because you were eating pizza with 'Sergeant Tony Sanchez and the guys' at the youth center, and when you got home you were too tired for anything except sleep."

"Stone, be fair . . ."

"Does he know you're married?"

"Of course he does."

"Is he?"

"Stone, stop it!"

"Is he married?"

"Yes!"

"Where do you eat all these pizzas?"

Her cheeks colored with anger. "At the club!"

"Yeah? Maybe I should surprise you with a visit one of these nights."

Her voice started to rise. "I would be very pleased if you did!"

"Really? Well, you know what, Dehan. I'd be pleased if you came home at night occasionally. You are a grown-up woman, and you are free to do exactly as you please in life, with me or with Tony. But you need to get your head out of that club just long enough to remember that you have a husband, you are married, and this..." I made a back-and-forth motion between us with my finger. "This is not how marriages work."

She frowned hard at me. "What the hell are you saying, Stone?"

I took a deep breath. "If you are developing feelings for Tony . . ." I paused because the name was like poison on my tongue. "Then you need to address that before things go any further."

Her jaw sagged. "You think . . ." She shook her head. "You can't possibly think . . ."

"Why? Why not?"

"But . . ."

"He's a good-looking guy, he has a likeable, engaging personality. He's a good, noble person, and he is passionate about his project and about helping the kids, just like you. Hell! He's your age! You probably have a lot more in common with him than you have with me. You certainly prefer spending your free time with him rather than with me."

She was shaking her head. "Stone, no . . ."

"Really?" I went to the dresser and opened a drawer. From it I took out a long, glossy envelope with a picture of a tropical beach on it. I carried it to the kitchen. "That cabin on the beach, on Espiritu Santo, in Vanuatu, is where we should have spent last night. The first of seven nights. It was your birthday present to me last November. Do you remember that? While we were supposed to be traveling, we were working. While we were supposed to be checking in, you were at the club, with Tony. And while we were supposed to be having oysters and champagne, you were eating pizza . . . with Tony. So now tell me, Dehan, that you don't prefer to spend your free time with Tony rather than with me."

She had gone pale, and there were tears in her eyes. "Stone, why didn't you remind me?"

"I can't lie to you, Dehan. I didn't remind you because I was so sick and tired of the damned project, and especially Tony, that I wanted to see if you would remember. You didn't."

"Stone, I am so sorry."

"I don't want you to be sorry, Dehan. I want you to be clear. If our relationship has run its course, then acknowledge it and tell me. We are both grown-ups, we both know how these situations play out. How long before the two of you are left alone having pizza one night . . . ?"

"No, Stone! I swear! Sure, I admire Tony for what he does, but I *do not* have those feelings for him! This is *not* about him! This is about the kids, Stone. You *have* to understand that!"

"I don't have to understand anything that you don't communicate to me, Dehan. And lately the only thing you communicate to me is that you have zero interest in spending time with me."

She drew breath to answer, but the doorbell rang. I glanced at my watch. Six thirty. I looked at Dehan and was aware of a growing anger in my belly.

"Is this Tony? Had you arranged for him to pick you up and forgot to tell me?"

She was still frowning and shook her head. "*No!*"

I went and pulled open the door. It was Mo. I scowled at him. "Mo? What the hell are you doing here? Do you know what time it is?"

"Yeah, Stone, I know what time it is. Is Carmen here?"

The anger I had been repressing suddenly flared up. The heat in my belly surged to my head. "Of course she's here! Where the hell do you think she'd be at six thirty in the morning?"

Dehan appeared at my side. "Good morning, Mo. What's going on?"

He eyed her a moment, then looked at me resentfully. "Take it easy, Stone. You gonna invite me in or what?"

I sighed and stood aside. "Yeah, sure. Come on in. You want some coffee?"

Dehan added, "I'm making pancakes. You want some breakfast?"

He hesitated, licked his lips, then said, "Just some coffee, white, three sugars."

She poured it for him, and he sat at the table, half-set for breakfast. He spoke to his cup.

"Look, sit down, will ya?"

We sat, and I scowled at him. "What the hell is it, Mo? Has something happened? You need help?"

He closed his eyes and shook his head.

"No, I don't need help. I had the late shift tonight. Couple of hours ago I was called to a homicide on Eastchester Bay."

I frowned. "Why? That's not in the Forty-Third."

"It's complicated. The crime scene was in the Forty-Fifth, so the boys from the Forty-Fifth were there. Jim Blakemore was lead. Victim was a cop, from the Forty-Fifth." He looked straight at Dehan. "Sergeant Tony Sanchez."

I watched her. She went pale and put her hands to her mouth. "Tony?" There were tears in her eyes. "What happened? Why did they call you?"

"He'd been shot, practically point-blank."

"What about his wife? Is she okay?"

His voice was wooden, and his face was hard. "She found him."

Dehan frowned. "Found him? Where? When we left the club he said he was going straight home."

"That's where he was found, at home."

"She wasn't there with him? Where was she?"

"Out with friends. She has an alibi, Carmen. You said you were at a club? You guys were pretty close, right?"

Dehan's frown deepened. So did mine. She said, "We weren't close, Mo. We were working on the same project at the *youth* club."

"Sure, so what time did you guys leave the club?"

She glanced at me, and I could see the first stirrings of fear in her eyes. "I don't know exactly. Nine thirty? I got home at what, ten?"

"Ten fifteen."

Mo's eyes darted from Dehan to me and back again. "So did you go straight home from the club? Or did you go on somewhere else?"

I snarled, "Take it easy, Mo. What are you driving at?"

I felt Dehan's hand on my arm. "We talked for ten minutes or so about what needed to be done today, and then I came straight home."

"And he told you he was going home, to his wife?"

"Of course. He didn't say, 'Okay, Carmen, now I'm going home to my wife . . .' but that was what I understood."

"What *did* he say?"

"Uh . . ." She closed her eyes to think, then shrugged her shoulders. "'Okay, I'm dead beat, I'm for home.' To which I replied, 'Yeah, me too.' He got in his car and I got in mine. I came home."

"Was there anybody else at the club?"

"No, everybody had left by then."

He held her eye, and I saw her breathing quicken and her cheeks color. He said, "What time did the last person leave the club before you left?"

Her eyes swiveled and met mine. She was fighting the tears. "About nine o'clock, maybe a little before that."

"So you were alone with Tony for maybe forty-five minutes."

"Half an hour or forty-five minutes, yes."

"What did you do during that time, Carmen?"

"Tony was in the office, doing the accounts, and I was cleaning up the club."

I put my hand on Dehan's arm and leaned forward.

"Okay, that's enough, Mo. Dehan isn't answering another

goddamn question until you tell us what the hell is going on here."

He stared at me like he was trying to work out what was wrong with me.

"What's going on? What's going on, John, is that as a courtesy, the Forty-Fifth has requested that a detective from the Forty-Third come and have a talk with Detective Carmen Dehan, about a murder. But not just any murder, the murder of a cop. Because the last person to see that cop alive, at nine thirty last night, was Carmen. And it so happens that for maybe forty-five minutes, they were alone together. So I am real interested to know what happened during those forty-five minutes."

"Cut the crap, Mo! Does Dehan need a lawyer?"

"I don't know! Does she?" He turned to Dehan. "Do you?"

"*Of course not!*" She scowled at Mo and then at me, trying to read my face. I don't know what she read there. I had no idea what I was feeling except rage. Dehan was speaking again. "Mo, this is ridiculous! You know me!"

He shook his head. "Uh-uh, sister. Nobody knows nobody. And you can be thankful they didn't send a couple of patrol cars to take you in!"

"I did not kill Tony!"

"Really?"

She leaned forward, her expression close to panic. "Of course not, Mo! I came straight home! Stone will tell you!"

"Yeah, but Stone wasn't with you at the club. From what I hear, you haven't seen a lot of Stone for the last three months. But you *have* been seeing an awful lot of Sergeant Sanchez, every night."

"At the club, Mo! With people everywhere!"

"Not last night."

"Come on, Mo! I saw him at the club. He went home and I went home. I did not kill Tony!"

"Well, if that's true, if you didn't shoot him, explain to me why the hell your prints are all over his gun, the gun that killed him."

"*What?*"

He shook his head. "I really hate to do this, but Carmen Stone, I am placing you under arrest for the murder of Sergeant Anthony Sanchez..."

CHAPTER 2

The chief, Inspector John Newman, looked queasy. He kept shaking his head and avoiding my eye from behind his desk.

"John," he kept saying, "you know how much I value you and Carmen. Not just as damned fine cops, but as friends. But I can't discuss this with you. You have a conflict of interests. You're compromised, John. You must see that. I have to hand her over to the Forty-Fifth."

"Sir, this is Dehan we are talking about. The idea that she would kill a fellow officer is not crazy, it's outlandish."

"I know! I know!" He raised his eyebrows high, hunched his shoulders, and gave his head quick little shakes. "But the law doesn't give a good goddamn about what we think, or what we know for that matter. The law is a process, John, you know that! And it is the same process for you, for me, and for Carmen. That's the rule of law."

"Sir, I am not asking you not to investigate her association with Sanchez—"

"The Forty-Fifth will investigate her association with Sanchez, John."

"Obviously they have to do that. And obviously I am not asking to be part of the investigation. Clearly that is out of the question. All I am asking is that you hold off on arresting her until you have more substantial evidence. Her fingerprints could have got on that gun any number of ways. She's interested in arms. She might have picked it up to look at it. Bottom line, sir, if you don't arrest her you don't have to hand her over to the Forty-Fifth."

He sighed and leaned his elbows on the table. "John, if I don't arrest her, the Forty-Fifth will. What would you do if she was not your wife and your partner? If you didn't know her? She was the last person to see him alive, they were alone for almost an hour, she had been spending increasing amounts of time with him for the last three months . . . And now he shows up dead, shot with his own revolver, at point-blank range, and her prints are all over the gun."

I sagged back in my chair. "There is one very obvious point, sir."

"Tell me."

"You have often said yourself that Dehan is an excellent cop. She is smart, and she is cool-headed."

"That's true, John. I have said it, and I maintain it."

"If she had shot Sergeant Sanchez, her prints would not be on the gun."

He smiled. It was a very sad expression. It said my argument smacked of desperation.

"People can act in very bizarre ways when they are . . . confused, or panicking. The arrest is proper and correct, John. We have made it clear to the DA that we do not oppose bail and that we do not believe she is a flight risk. What Detective Blakemore will have to say about that, we will have to wait and see. The most you can hope for is a modest bail. I am very sorry."

I nodded. I knew he was right, and there was damn all I could do about it.

"Can I at least have a copy of the case file?"

"That would be very irregular, John."

"Goddamn it, sir! This is my wife! One of the best detectives at the precinct! We owe her that much! Mo has made up his mind that Dehan is guilty, when you and I both know she isn't!"

He sat in silence for a good fifteen seconds before he leaned forward and flipped a switch on his desk.

"Bring me a copy of the Sergeant Anthony Sanchez case file." Then he sat back and laced his fingers over his belly.

"Sanchez was found shot to death in his bed, by his wife, at twelve thirty last night. She's a Realtor and an entrepreneur, Astrid Meyer, and she had been out with colleagues celebrating a big deal they had pulled off. Exactly what happened is not very clear right now, but the doors onto the backyard were open, and it seems the killer fled that way."

"Sir, Dehan left him at the club . . ."

"That's her story, John, but so far it is uncorroborated. She says they were alone, at the club, for about forty-five minutes or an hour before she went home. That's enough time for her to get from the club to Sanchez's house, kill him, and get back to Morris Park by ten fifteen. It is feasible, Stone, that when the last member of the club had left, Carmen and Sergeant Sanchez went back to his house."

"That's insane!" A wave of nausea washed over me. "Dehan would not do that!"

He gazed at me with very sad eyes. "Nobody would do it, John. And yet, it happens all the time. We humans have very little control over what we do. You know that. When passion strikes . . ."

"She has too much integrity . . ." I said it, and in my head I was hearing our argument that morning. "And, even if she had fallen for him, why would she kill him?"

"We don't know that she did, John. But we have to investigate the possibility, and we need to know exactly what time they left the club. We have men on that even as we speak."

There was a tap on the door, and a uniform leaned in and

handed the inspector a slim manila file, then left again. The inspector dropped the file in front of me.

"You may have mistakenly got the impression that I had given you permission to take this file. If you did, I didn't notice you take it. Obviously it is impossible for you to investigate this case, as you cannot be objective about it, neither will you be able to work on another case while Carmen is being investigated. So, I advise you to take a couple of weeks' paid leave until this is all over."

"Thank you, sir."

I went to stand. "John?"

"Yes, sir?"

"Under no circumstances are you to undertake a private investigation of this case."

"I won't, sir."

The phone rang. He grabbed it, and I stood.

"Yes, Inspector Newman here . . ." He raised a hand, telling me to wait. "Yes, ma'am, Carmen Stone." He listened for a while. "They both have a superb record, ma'am, outstanding. Ethnicity?" He frowned. "Part Mexican and part Jewish, is that relevant, ma'am?" He nodded and rolled his eyes. "Yes, of course, I see that. The victim was a white male, ma'am . . . indeed . . . a police officer . . . Thank you, ma'am, I will tell her husband. Good day to you too."

He put down the phone. "The DA. John, bail is set at twenty-five thousand dollars. Can you post that now?"

I nodded. "Thank you, sir."

"You know that normally in a case like this you would have to wait for the hearing, and bail would be much higher."

"I know that, sir."

"The DA knows Carmen, or at least thinks she does, and is willing to . . ." He drew breath, searching for words that would not imply something untoward. I said, "I understand, sir. I'll go and get her."

"Yes, go and get her, John. And, John?"

I paused with my hand on the door. "Yes, sir?"

"You'd better find out what the hell happened. Fix this."

I nodded and left.

Downstairs I sorted out her bail. Then I went to our desks in the detectives' room and collected our personal effects. Mo's desk was just across from ours, but he wouldn't look at me. I didn't say anything to him either. I collected our stuff and went to wait outside on the steps, watching the incessant rain and listening to it patter.

Fifteen minutes later she came out and stood staring at me a moment. Then she hunched her shoulders, walked down the steps, and crossed the road to where my ancient, burgundy Jag was parked. I followed her, unlocked the car, and we climbed in and slammed the doors. She sat a moment wiping the rain from her face with a paper towel.

We drove in silence, heading slowly back toward home. For a while the only sound was the incessant squeak and thud of the wipers. When we had turned off Story and onto White Plains I said, "I think you need to explain a few things to me."

"Like what?"

"Well, we could start with, what the hell is going on?"

"I don't know."

"Followed by, what the *hell* has been going on for the last three months?"

She sighed and closed her eyes. When she spoke, she articulated very precisely and very carefully.

"Nothing has been going on. I saw the flier on the board at the station asking for volunteers for a youth club to help kids get on the straight and narrow. I called and got involved. I got too involved. But I got too involved with the *kids,* not with Tony! Tony was a nice guy, but I had absolutely no feelings for him, Stone. What I cared about, and what I was involved with, was the jeet kune do classes I was teaching the kids. Nothing more. I don't know how you can think . . ."

I cut her dead. "Don't. We can't do that. You're a prime suspect in a homicide investigation, and your prints are all over the murder weapon. We need to stay cool and focused, and I need to know the truth."

"I'm telling you the truth, Stone!"

"All of it!"

"Yes, all of it!"

"I need to hear you say it. I need you to look me in the eye and I need to hear you say it."

She stared at me. The windshield wipers squeaked on the glass, steady and rhythmic. Outside the downpour hissed. I stopped at a red light and turned to face her.

"Did you at any time have an affair with Tony Sanchez—and by that I include a secret cuddle and a kiss!"

She shouted the answer at me, balling her fists: "*No!*"

"Was the relationship between you, on either side, his or yours, ever anything more than professional?"

"No, never!"

"Did you go to his house yesterday, or last night?"

"No, absolutely not."

A honk behind me told me the lights had changed. I put the old Mark II in gear and moved off. She was watching me, waiting for the next question.

"Did you kill him?"

"No, Stone. I did not kill Tony Sanchez."

"How did your prints get on his gun?"

This time she took longer to reply. I glanced at her. She was staring out at the rain. Finally she said, "I don't know."

"That's not good enough. We can't have secrets, Dehan. If you're done with me and you want to move on . . ."

She turned and almost screamed at me. "*I am not done with you and I do not want to move on! Stop saying that!*"

I let her finish, then went on. "Even if you were, you can start keeping secrets after, but you are looking at spending the rest of your life in prison, Dehan. You cannot afford to keep secrets from me. Not now."

Her voice was quiet. "Not now, not ever."

"Then why the long, thoughtful pause when I asked about the prints?"

"Because I am trying to work out how they got there."

Neither of us talked again until we turned onto Morris Park Avenue. The clouds were so dense overhead that the streetlamps were on and the cars had their headlamps on even though it was midmorning. The traffic was slow moving, and the water looked an inch deep on the blacktop. Dehan finally asked me, "Do you believe me?"

"Of course I do. I just needed to hear you say it." I hesitated. "It's the first thing I've heard you say in three months that wasn't either work related or, 'I'm beat, I'm going to bed.'"

She sighed. "You made your point, Stone. I'm sorry."

I gave my head a brief shake. "I don't want your apology. I want you to understand that bad things happen to relationships when the communication breaks down."

She didn't answer for a while, then put her hand on my arm and said, "Yes."

"So, somebody is trying to frame you."

She made a face like brain-ache. "But, who? I'm sitting here going through all the people at the club one by one, trying to work out how the hell they got my prints onto that gun, and why in the name of all that is holy they would want to frame me!"

I grunted. "Wrong question, Little Grasshopper."

"Yeah? So what is the right question?"

"Who wanted Tony dead—aside from me, of course."

She flashed a look at me. "Stone! Don't even joke about that!"

"Who says I'm joking?" I said sourly. "In any case, setting me aside, focus on the question. Who wanted Tony dead?"

"Okay." She nodded. "That makes sense. Framing me could be opportunism. So who would want him dead?"

I turned into Haight Avenue and pulled up outside our house. The lights were still on from that morning, when Dehan had been led away. The limpid glow from the living-room window made wet highlights on the sidewalk. I turned to face Dehan.

"It's three months, Dehan, and whatever you say, you got to know him pretty well in that time. You must have heard him make phone calls, you must have seen him talk to people, he must have made a hundred comments—a thousand!—that at the time meant nothing to you, and you disregarded them. Now you have to make your mind go back over those three months again, every minute of them, with a fine-tooth comb. You have to sift through every word that he said. What other relationships did he have? How did he get on with his wife?"

The rain drummed on the roof of the car. The windshield filled with droplets, and the lonely, quiet street vanished into an abstract of fractured light. Somewhere outside the dark cocoon of the cab I could hear the slap and patter of water overflowing from a gutter. Dehan's voice came quiet in the shadows.

"Stone, I'll try, but whether you believe me or not, we never talked about personal stuff. We talked about the club." She reached out and took hold of my hand. "If I was unfaithful to you, it was with the kids who wanted a better shot at life, the ones who wanted to escape from the gangs, learn to fight the good fight."

I nodded, understanding perhaps better than she did right then what she was telling me.

"Okay, let's go inside and get out of this rain. We have a lot of work to do, Dehan. We are fighting for our lives, and failure just isn't an option."

We sat a moment longer in the gloom, looking at each other. Then, very quietly, she said, "Okay."

We got out of the car, locked it, and ran, hunched into our shoulders, across the sidewalk and up the stairs to the front door. I turned the key in the latch, she pushed, and I went in behind her and slammed the door closed behind us. Then we were standing, dripping wet, just a few inches away from each other. Her hair clung in wet strands to her cheeks and brow. Her eyes, huge and dark, searched my face. Her hands went up to my face, and her fingers stroked my cheeks.

"Stone," she whispered the word, "there has never been anyone but you. There never will be. I am so sorry I made you go through this."

I drew breath to answer, but what happened next made all words unnecessary.

CHAPTER 3

We showered, and while she made an early lunch, I made a fire. We didn't need a fire; it wasn't cold. It was muggy. But there was an unspoken agreement that we needed the comfort of the fire.

Neither of us was very hungry, so she made mini DIY pizzas with bread rolls, tomato, cheese, herbs, and salami and we cracked a couple of beers. After that we sat at the table, where it was still half-set for breakfast, and ate in silence. When Dehan had put the last piece of toast, cheese, and tomato in her mouth, and was licking her fingers, she said:

"Astrid Sanchez, though professionally she goes by her maiden name, Astrid Meyer. She inherited a realty business from her father, whose great-grandfather emigrated from Germany as a child with his parents. They all worked real hard and became prosperous Realtors, family business. Mom died when Astrid was a kid, Dad kept things together, strong, authoritarian, German patriarch type. He wasn't thrilled that his daughter was going to marry a Latino, but at least he was a cop. Then he—Dad—died of cancer so the issue became academic."

I waited till she'd finished, then asked, "He told you all this? I thought you only discussed the club."

She grinned. "I never realized you were so jealous, Stone. This is a new side to your character."

"You never gave me reason to be before. I'm at home eating alone out of a can, and going over cold-case files, while this guy is telling you his life story."

"No, that's not what happened, and he didn't tell me all that. You asked me to piece things together. That's what I did. Remember, I wasn't the only volunteer there. There were also a couple of guys from the Forty-Fifth. I guess they were pals because they talked about everything, and I couldn't help overhearing. Sometimes I think they forgot I was there. Anyway, that's what I pieced together."

"She ever visit the club?"

She nodded. "Yeah. She told me once she liked to think of her family as philanthropists. I know she often discussed the tax breaks of putting money into the club with Tony. She came to visit several times."

"You didn't like her."

She spread her hands and raised her shoulders. It was an oddly Italian gesture. "Like?" she said. "She wasn't important enough to *dis*like, Stone. I wasn't interested. I didn't care. I had a dojo, I had a gym, I had thirty kids from age five to age fifteen, and they all wanted to learn Bruce Lee's secrets of self-control, and how to overcome limitations. Ask me their names. I know every single one of them. Ask me about their home lives, about their parents, about their brothers and what gangs they're in. I know every detail. But Astrid Meyer? She wasn't why I was there, Stone. And neither, for that matter, was Tony."

I smiled. "Okay, I believe you, Dehan, you don't have to keep proving it to me."

"Good." She paused a moment. "And I'm sorry you had to eat alone going over cold-case files. I should have been aware of that."

I smiled. "Yesterday's rain," I said, and in response the wind lashed the kitchen window, and the trees in the backyard nodded and bowed.

She stared a moment, out at the darkening afternoon, then down at her empty plate.

"Anyhow, Tony was this kind of angel, devoting all his time to good works, helping the kids, preserving the environment of the bay, you name it, he was involved. And his wife, who made stacks of money, was always there supporting him financially—or at least talking about it—and, I guess, to some extent, taking the credit. They have—had—a big house on the bay, Bayshore Drive. Her father bought two houses and knocked them into one, right next to the Huntington Woods."

"You ever been?"

"No, Stone, I have never been."

"So what about other women, Dehan? Were there any girls or women who were interested in this angel, whom he seemed close to, or who wanted to get close to him?"

She sighed and sagged.

"It is so hard to answer that, Stone. I have this huge motivation to say yes, because if there was, maybe I escape spending the next thirty years in prison. But am I being honest and objective? I don't know!"

"So, that's what we have cops for, and lawyers and courts, to test the evidence. If there is a possibility that one or more women were interested in him, or if there is a chance he was having an affair, we need to look into it, even if only to discard it, however uncomfortable that may be for you."

"It's not uncomfortable." She lifted her hands, palm up, then dropped them on the table again. "It wasn't just boys who went to the club. Girls went too. Tony was fun, likeable, and I guess he was good-looking, so a lot of girls used to hang around him. And he was a good guy, so I guess they felt safe with him. You know? For a girl growing up in the rough parts of the Bronx, feeling safe with a guy can be a big deal."

I waited, and after a moment I asked, "So?"

"So, does that mean he was having an affair with one of them? I don't think so, but maybe he was."

"The opportunities were there?"

She nodded. "Yeah, the opportunities were there."

"That's important."

"I know."

"You can't protect this guy, Dehan."

"I'm not protecting him." I didn't answer, and after a moment she had to fill the silence. "He was a good guy, Stone. Okay? I didn't feel anything romantic or sexual for him, but I liked him. He was a rare, honorable human being in a cruel, selfish world. And if he is dead, then his memory should not be sullied, because his memory can continue to help those kids."

"Okay, I understand, but we need to get past that point."

"What do you mean?"

"I mean you are fighting for your life. The clock is ticking, and you are already running out of time. You cannot afford to worry about protecting Tony's memory. Because the price for protecting his memory could be thirty years in jail. Get past it, and start thinking about what women—we need their names and addresses—what women he might have been sleeping with."

"Jesus, Stone!"

"Three months was quite enough. I don't want to lose you for another thirty years. Let's get real, Dehan!"

"Look, Stone, he was just an idealistic guy who wanted to do something for the kids in the Bronx. He worked hard, and in the evenings he would go home, sometimes with his wife, sometimes alone."

"How do you know he went home?"

She shrugged. "I don't, but people talk. Especially if an upright person who is trying to set an example starts to stray. People talk. But nobody ever talked or gossiped about him. And like I said, he always left alone if he didn't leave with his wife."

I nodded. "Okay, Dehan, we're going to get an attorney and we're going to get you off these charges. We'll get them dropped or we'll get the case thrown out."

"How?"

"Because we'll discover the truth." I gave it a moment, then said, "This is the last time I am going to raise this subject. But I have to say this, for both our sakes. You don't have to tell me everything—at least, not yet—but when you meet with your attorney..."

"*My* attorney? Not *our* attorney?"

I nodded. "That's my point. You don't have to tell me everything, but you will have to tell *him* everything, in detail, warts and all. Do you understand? Because if you lie to protect me or my feelings, or somebody else you care about, whatever lies you tell will come back to haunt you down the line."

She looked weary, and there were deep shadows under her eyes. She stared at the tabletop for a long time, then raised her eyes to meet mine.

"Enough, Stone. Enough already. I am telling you everything, and I am going to tell *our* attorney everything, A, because you are my husband and I love you and I have no secrets from you! And B, because I am smart and I know how this works. Enough already! I think I have earned your trust by now!"

My cell rang. I picked it up and answered, "Stone..."

There was a brief silence. Then Joe, from the lab, said, "John, I am not calling you. This call never happened. I'm in a phone booth, and I have to make this quick."

"What is it, Joe?"

"I've been putting in my own time on the Sergeant Sanchez case. The whole house was dusted for prints, and I have analyzed the results personally."

My heart was pounding and my belly was hot. I controlled my voice and said, "What did you find?"

"Carmen was there, John."

"That's got to be a mistake."

"How many times do you think I checked it? Her prints are on the banisters to the upper floor, on the doorjamb and the frame, they are on the windowsill and on the foot of the bed and the bedhead. There is no mistake, John. Carmen's prints are all over that room. The room where he was killed."

I was quiet for a long moment, then said, "Okay, thanks, Joe."

I hung up and sat staring at the phone. Dehan was watching me and finally said, "You'd better tell me what that was about, Stone."

"Your prints."

"What about them?"

"They are at Sergeant Sanchez's house."

"*What?*"

"They are on the banisters going up to the bedrooms. They are on the doorframe and the doorjamb, and they are all over the bed, the foot of the bed and the head."

She stood suddenly and shouted across the table at me.

"*For Christ's sake, Stone!*"

She strode across the room toward the bay window, one hand on her hip, the other running fingers through her hair. She turned toward me and shouted again, her face beginning to collapse into tears.

"*I did not kill Tony! I was never at Tony's house! I did not have an affair with Tony! I wouldn't!*"

I stood and went to her, and put my arms around her and kissed the top of her head.

"I trust you because I know you are good and loyal and faithful. But above all, Dehan, you're the best cop I have ever known."

She raised her damp face to look up into mine.

"Thanks," she said with a damp voice, "but what's that got to do with anything?"

I pointed to her leather jacket hanging on the back of her chair.

"Go reach in your right pocket. Pull out what's inside." She did as I said and stood a moment staring at the blue latex gloves in her hand. I went on. "As soon as he said your prints were on the banister, I knew. Then when he said the doorframe and the jamb, and the bed . . . I knew it couldn't be you. You would never make such a stupid, elementary mistake, especially knowing that you always carry gloves and evidence bags. If you'd done it, they'd never have caught you."

I sighed and rested my ass against the back of the sofa.

"But, Dehan, unless you were there on some earlier occasion and you don't remember..."

"Don't be ridiculous."

"Then we are up against a very skilled operator who understands forensics and is very determined to put you in the frame."

She stared at me for a long moment, and her face was very pale.

"Who the hell would want to do this to me?"

"Not you." I shook my head. "*Him*. Get this clear in your head. You are a convenient scapegoat. *He* is the intended victim. You need to think, kiddo. If the killer was aware enough of you to select you as a scapegoat, you are aware enough of him to know who he is."

She nodded slowly. "... Okay ..."

"Now, I am going to phone Saul Cohen..."

Her face flushed. "We can't afford Saul Cohen, Stone! Besides, the guy is a rat! He's on the payroll of every Mafia in New York!"

I nodded as I dialed. "And you know why? Because he's the best. I'll sell the Jag, I'll mortgage the house. I'll do whatever we need to do, Dehan. We have to beat this rap..."

A female voice that sounded like it had spent the morning being rubbed by a whetstone sliced in, "Cohen and Cohen Attorneys, how can I help you?"

"Yeah, I need to talk to Saul, Saul Cohen, tell him..."

"Have you an appointment?"

"I don't need one. Tell him it's Detective John Stone..."

"Detective Stone, perhaps I wasn't clear. Mr. Cohen is extremely busy. He is not able to simply drop what he is doing and..."

"Let me explain what is going to happen, sister," I growled into the phone. "First, when Saul finds out you failed to put me through he is going to be *very* upset with you. After that he is going to spend the next ten years apologizing to me for not having made you aware of me, and you are going to spend the next ten years doing everything and anything he tells you, trying to make up for the very *big* mistake you are about to make. Now, quit wasting my time and put me through to Saul!"

After five minutes, Saul Cohen's deep, smooth rumble oozed down the line.

"John, I am not quite sure what's going on. I was about to tell Maggie to tell you to go to hell, but the message was so totally not you, that curiosity got the better of me."

I put the cell on speaker and laid it on the table.

"My wife, Carmen Dehan..."

"I know of her, the cold cases you both run, damn fine cop. What about her? Don't tell me you're getting divorced! I don't do divorces, Stone."

"Shut up, Saul. She's being framed for the murder of a cop."

"Ho! Ho, ho, ho! Is it Christmas? Was I a good boy? *Man!* So what? You want me to represent her? Tell me you want me to represent her!"

"Yeah, that's what I want. Will you do it?"

"*Do it?* Are you crazy? Have you any idea how much this is going to hurt the NYPD? I am going to drag them kicking and screaming through the mire, and then I am going to feed them their own..."

"Saul! How much is this going to cost?"

"Seriously?"

"Quit being a pain in the ass, Saul. How much?"

"I want the exclusive rights to write and publish the book."

"We'll talk."

"You're not wrong. We'll talk. And if you give me a hard time you can run your own defense." He laughed. "The NYPD goes after one of its own! The blameless, virtuous cold-case couple, Stone and Dehan, turn to the loveably wicked Saul Cohen, savior of evil Mafiosi from Maine to San Diego, darling of the Mafia, brother to the Devil himself, and he and Stone battle courageously together, brothers-in-arms, to save the virtuous Carmen. Man, I cannot *wait* to get my hands on this case. Where are you?"

"The Bronx..."

"Where did the crime take place?"

"Eastchester Bay."

"Eastchester Bay? I have heard mutterings. They're trying to keep a lid on it. So that was your wife, Carmen? I'm at my house on Oyster Bay right now. Hold on, I'm going to get back to you. I'll call you on this number in five minutes."

He hung up, and we sat staring at each other across the table. After a moment Dehan said, "Even if he gets me off, Stone, this will be the end of my career as a cop. The cop who used Saul Cohen to humiliate the NYPD and the Forty-Third."

"We're fighting for our lives."

"I'm not saying we're wrong. I'm saying it will cost us our careers."

I shrugged. "So we'll open a firm of private investigators. I'll be Nero Wolfe and you can be Archie Goodwin. We'll have to move to Manhattan and buy a brownstone."

"Stone, I am serious."

"So am I."

I was about to say something about crossing bridges when we came to them and the phone rang.

"Yeah, Stone."

"It's Saul. I'm booking a suite at the Bay View on Country Club Road. You know it? I'll set up an operations room there. We'll have breakfast tomorrow at nine. Bring *everything*. You're a good cop, so is she. You know what I need. Conference at nine sharp."

He had hung up again before I had a chance to thank him.

And I really wanted to thank him.

Scan the QR code below to purchase IN HOT BLOOD.
Or go to: righthouse.com/in-hot-blood

Printed in Dunstable, United Kingdom